The Rancher's
Ultimatum

Published by Phaze Books

PHAZE
Cincinnati, Ohio

The Rancher's Ultimatum

a novel of erotic romance by

NIA K. FOXX

The Rancher's Ultimatum copyright 2006, 2007 by Nia K. Foxx

Cincinnati, Ohio

A Phaze Production
Phaze Books
6470A Glenway Avenue, #109
Cincinnati, OH 45211-5222
Phaze is an imprint of Mundania Press, LLC.

To order additional copies of this book, contact:
books@phaze.com
www.Phaze.com

Cover art © 2006,Kathryn Lively
Edited by Kathryn Lively

Trade Paperback ISBN-13: 978-1-59426-743-7
Trade Paperback ISBN-10: 1-59426-743-X

First Edition – August, 2007
Printed in the United States of America

10 9 8 7 6 5 4 3 2 1

Prologue

Her body was so alive with pleasure, it sizzled. Lynn's lover secured the second manacle on her wrist above her head, leaving the cuffs loose enough to prevent chafing to her almond colored skin.

"Beautiful," he uttered, admiring her prone form. Strong fingers traced over the generous curves of her body. Full hips, thick thighs, and plump breasts received the most attention.

His immediate absence was felt as he left the bed momentarily, only to return with a deep, wooden bowl. She strained to see its contents, knowing whatever the container held was meant for her pleasure.

"Patience," her gruff voiced lover instructed, a smug grin spread across perfect lips. Honeyed eyes studied her from behind his black mask. With eyes like that, she knew the rest of him had to be gorgeous. If only he'd remove the mask. God, how she hated that thing, wanted nothing more but to rip the silk material off and finally reveal the face of her mystery lover.

For six months he'd come to her the same way each night, slipping quietly through her window, which was no easy feat considering her bedroom was on the second floor. His muscular upper body was barely concealed by the unbuttoned leather vest he wore. Black jeans hung low on his hips, shaping the tight ass she'd only had the pleasure of glimpsing when he finally stripped away the detested articles of clothing.

He extracted a lone ice cube from the bowl, wetting it between his lips before gliding the chilled substance from her navel, up her soft abdomen to one breast. He circled the nipple and it puckered instantly from the frigid cube. The ice melted against her warm skin, allowing a trail of cool water to trickle down one breast. Ever attentive, her lover promptly slurped up the liquid, allowing his tongue to follow the path up to her dark nub.

Lynn groaned, arching into his mouth when he suckled her flesh.

"Do you like that?" he mumbled around the nipple.

"Yes."

He let the aroused nugget pop from his mouth. "Good, cause there's more of where that came from." His sexy Texan drawl was almost lyrical.

Her other nipple was treated to the same frosty delight, which caused her to nearly explode with pleasure. By the time he'd finished with her twin peaks she was squirming all over her queen-sized bed, begging for more. She waited with baited breath as he left the mattress to undress. To her surprise the Stetson was the first to go, revealing thick, wavy brown hair she'd never seen before. The vest followed next, exposing a golden, well-formed chest. She bit her lip in anticipation, waiting for him to discard his pants like he'd done every night, only this time her lover paused.

"I think it's time."

"What?" she asked confused. If he meant it was time to get his sexy ass back in bed she agreed wholeheartedly, but dared not voice her thoughts. He was one hundred percent in control, and she was happy to relent to his domination.

"Wouldn't you like to see who you've been making love to all these months?"

Her heart pounded in her chest, she couldn't believe it. Did she really want to know, to have the mystery end? Yes, she decided, it was time to put a face and name with that luscious body.

Afraid to use words she merely nodded, watching intently as the mask was removed with a flourish, revealing the devilishly handsome face of Jake Rangell.

* * * *

"Damn, damn," Lynn exclaimed, coming to a jerky wakefulness. Beside her, the alarm clock buzzed in its annoyingly high-pitched fashion daring to be ignored.

"Jake Rangell!" She punched her pillow. Of all the men to have erotic dreams about, why did it have to be him?

Just a dream, she repeated to herself. She'd thought her dreams were the one place she could live out her submissive fantasies without embarrassment, and who should happen to play her leading man but him. The one man she'd secretly had a crush on since…well, for as long as she could remember.

Understandably, a bit of reality would manifest itself in her subconscious dream world, she surmised, easing out of bed. Yet, the fact she continued to harbor feelings for Jake these many years only added a level of resentment to her warring emotions. After all, if it weren't for him her family wouldn't be in their current predicament. Hell, if she'd dreamed of an axe murderer last night Jake would have been the psycho wielding the weapon. *Certainly he couldn't be same man who visited her all those other nights.*

No, his presence was directly related to the meeting that loomed ahead of her that day, nothing more. Well, if everything went as planned, her family's ranch would be saved and she wouldn't have to worry about any special appearances by Jake Rangell in future dreams.

One

"I'd never thought the day would come again when a Harrington would grace the home of a Rangell," the large man behind the massive oak desk spoke after several still moments.

"Technically I'm not a Harrington, as we both know," Lynn supplied, grateful that the awkward silence had finally been broken. Nothing had prepared her for the shock of seeing Jake again after eleven years. Time had been more than kind to him. At thirty-nine, his brownish blond hair was just beginning to show flecks of silver. Caramel eyes were still framed by thick lashes as she'd remembered, although the crinkles at their corners were new. It all served to add a distinguishing air to him.

Like most ranchers, his skin was sun bronzed, but unlike a majority it hadn't succumbed to the leathery look of years spent under the grueling Texas sun. He wore his hair a little longer than she remembered, its thick strands waving just over his ears. Bangs hung about half an inch from his brows. He was much broader than she recalled, too. His muscular forearms and biceps were evident in the short-sleeved, black T-shirt he wore, a far cry from the staunch business suit-clad men she'd become accustomed to dealing with over the years since her move to Arizona.

Lynn took a deep breath, recalling the reason for the visit, the outcome of which would mean the end or continuance of her family's ranch.

"So, what brings you to Rangell Ranch?"

"I wanted to speak with you about a business arrangement. First, I should say I've reviewed the land contracts you signed with my brothers and found them to be far from equitable, but I'm hoping we can put that behind us with what I propose today."

"Not equitable?"

"Yes, it would seem that neither Ryan nor Logan were fully aware of the implications of their agreement with you."

"I'm not sure why, everything was outlined in the contract."

"Which was over thirty pages long and filled with enough legalese to confuse even the savviest of attorneys."

"But it seems you managed to translate the document well enough. Perhaps they should have hired a better lawyer," Jake returned with the ease of a man aware that he had the upper hand. He looked relaxed in the sleek leather chair, arms resting comfortably on his desk while his fingers drummed a silent tune.

"They didn't have an attorney review it at all," she admitted, still unable to believe Ryan's folly, one of many she'd discovered.

"Well that is unfortunate. Perhaps next time they'll seek the advice of legal counsel before entering into a *binding* contractual agreement, or at the very least have their baby sister do some ciphering for them."

Lynn bit back her reply, she'd never been one to let emotions get the best of her in business, but there was nothing ordinary about the situation. The Harringtons and Rangells were enemies, had been since her childhood, and the fact that she sat in front of Jake Rangell preparing to ingratiate herself on behalf of the Harringtons did not sit well with her. Yet, something needed to be done or her stepfather's ranch would be ruined. She'd just wished that her two older stepbrothers had bothered to call on her for help before things got to this point.

"As unfair as the contracts were, I'm not here to argue the merits of them with you." She was proud at how cool she managed to sound.

"Good. So what exactly are you here for?"

"Equipment. My brothers and I would like to lease some of the drilling machinery we haven't had success in obtaining on our own. It's nothing more than what you have on supply at that dried out well. I'm sure they will serve us all better in use than just sitting around collecting dust."

"Done a little trespassing, I see?"

"Not at all, enough of our lands neighbor each other and men do talk," she offered as an excuse.

"Exactly what type of equipment are we talking about?"

"It's all outlined here." Prepared for that question, Lynn took out an itemized list of things they still needed to continue drilling on the land her brother's hadn't been swindled out of by Jake. She slid the computer-generated list over his high glossed desk. The movement had her leaning across the expanse to reach him.

Jake's large fingers brushed her own in the exchange, and Lynn could have sworn the air-conditioned room felt suddenly hot.

"So, you think there's oil on The Harrington?" he said absently while skimming her list.

She nodded. "We've accomplished a lot over the months but have run into some barriers obtaining certain equipment."

"Yes, I've noticed the vast improvements since your return, the Harringtons are very lucky to call you family."

"As am I."

"I'm sure you've had to sink a lot of capital into the ranch for the upgrades and equipment you've gotten thus far. I must say it was looking rather shabby until you came home."

Lynn didn't bother to reply. It was common knowledge that if she hadn't come home when she did The Harringtons' ranch would still be in the sorry state she'd found upon her return. The infusion of her savings and crafty money management pulled them out of the red, paid off most of their creditors while affording them to go ahead with Phase One of their project. Unfortunately, the price their distributors came back with on the equipment they would need for Phase Two was short of highway robbery. There was no way they could lease, let alone buy, the items needed, have money for payroll, and cover general expenses.

"We're prepared to pay you above market for the lease of your equipment, which I believe is more than fair," she continued.

"That confident, are you?"

"Logan is, and that's enough for me." Logan Harrington was the youngest brother of the Harrington brood, and while he never had a penchant for business, one thing he did know was land. Surveying, excavation, drilling, you name it— Logan was the go-to guy.

"Well, it sounds like you all are on the right track. Unfortunately, I can't help you."

Lynn masked her disbelief. She'd plotted everything out so carefully, prepared a package that even a man with Jake's wealth couldn't balk at, or so she thought.

"Did you see the figures I've highlighted? We're prepared to pay above market to lease your equipment, at the already inflated rates you would stand to gain a bundle." And if he agreed it would still be much cheaper than the distributor's prices, she added quietly. He didn't need to know everything.

"I already have more money than I can spend. Besides, you're a business woman, what sense would it make for me to provide potential competitors with equipment regardless of the immediate gain?"

"Jake, we're not any competition to the enterprise you have going on here, we're just looking to keep The Harrington up and running. Ultimately we're a cattle ranch, you know that, and it's all we really want to be."

"And I wish you all the luck. Unfortunately, I can't help you."

He rose slowly. Worn denim jeans clung to his long legs, and her eyes stretched with him, taking in the tall imposing figure that was Jake Rangell.

"Can't or won't?" Lynn challenged, rising to her own five-foot, eight inch frame.

"Does it matter? Frankly I'm surprised that you would even come to me for help, with the obvious tension that has existed between our families."

"That all happened over twenty-four years ago. Your parents and my mother are dead now, why can't we just let that die with them?"

Lynn saw the sudden flash of anger in his eyes and realized that she'd obviously touched a nerve. The Harrington/Rangell feud started when she was just six years old. At the time, her mother, Kathleen James, worked in the Rangell household. Lynn's biological father was a foreman who died in a drilling accident while working on the ranch. After his death, the Rangells kept her mother in their employ as family cook and nanny for their only child, Jake. The arrangement worked well until some six months after her father's death, when Tom Rangell began making unwarranted advances towards his widowed employee.

Lynn could remember the intimate touches her mother would deflect when she thought no one else noticed. Everything came to a head after Tom tried forcing himself on her mother while his own wife was away visiting relatives. If a very strapping, teenaged Jake hadn't responded to the shrill cries of

Lynn, she was certain her mother would have fallen victim to Tom's lustful obsession.

Remorseful, Tom promised Kathleen the moon if she would continue working for him. Her mother promptly refused the suggestion and hurriedly packed up their meager belongings. Lynn recalled the grueling walk from the ranch, which was thankfully shortened when a passing ranch hand offered to take them the remainder of the way to town. Unfortunately, that was only the beginning of their hardships since her mother underestimated the Rangell reach and determination. Door after door was closed in her face despite the years she and her husband had spent in the community. Kathleen found herself blacklisted, with no means to leave the town or support her bewildered six-year-old.

Race Harrington met the mother and daughter in town as they were literally being escorted out of the local diner where Lynn's mother inquired about a help wanted sign. For two days since leaving Rangell ranch, mother and daughter spent their nights in the local bus station and days looking for Kathleen a job. Race's own wife had died two years earlier, leaving him to care for his two unruly sons. According to him, he was in desperate need of a woman's touch in his male dominated household. He offered Kathleen employment in exchange for room/board and a monthly wage that was unheard of at that time. She remembered her mother thinking over the offer while Race treated them to the best meal they'd had since leaving Rangell Ranch. In the end she accepted the position.

Upon hearing of her new job, Tom Rangell stormed The Harrington and demanded that Race dismiss his new employee, accusing her of stealing from his family home. When Race refused, Tom had the police pay a visit to his distant neighbor's ranch, but was unable to substantiate his claim of theft, forcing the charges to be dropped. Over the next months Tom would volley between trying to win the affections of her mother and smearing her name through the mud whenever she refused him. Kathleen became a virtual recluse on the ranch to avoid the scrutiny of the townspeople, devoting her time to her daughter, and the Harrringtons: Logan, Ryan, and Race.

As Kathleen would later explain to her, the closeness opened doors the two adults would have normally not thought to venture through in the Texas town. One morning, nearly a year after mother and daughter had taken up residence in the Harrington home, the children were gathered for a family meeting and informed that their parents were getting married, to each other. Ryan, the older of the two Harrington brothers, protested the marriage vehemently although he had an obvious affection for Kathleen, but Race immediately squelched his son's objections. In a quiet weekend ceremony, Lynn gained a stepfather and two step-brothers, whom she'd grown to adore.

From that point forward Tom Rangell directed his anger at anything Harrington. It was rumored that he never touched his wife after Race and Kathleen's marriage, so fixated was he on the newlyweds. His wife succumbed to cancer some five years later, which seemed to infuriate him even further to see the happy couple in public while he was left alone.

* * * *

"Again, Ms. James, I'm sorry, but there is nothing I can do," Jake enunciated each word, arms folded across the wide expanse of his chest.

His words brought her back in the moment. "Look Jake, this is really important to us, I wouldn't bother you if it weren't. Perhaps we can work out some other arrangement?" She tucked a lock of short brown hair behind her ear. "A portion of the proceeds?" Lynn offered.

"Thank you, but no."

"There has to be something." She hated the pleading note in her voice, but desperate times called for desperate measures.

"I'm afraid not. Now, if you'll excuse me."

He stepped around the wide desk, stopping at the entrance of his office while he waited for her to precede him out the door.

Concerned now that her window of opportunity was slipping away, she hurried on, "Please Jake, it would kill Race to lose his ranch."

"And why should that be important to me?" he asked none-too-gently.

"Because I know you. You're a kind person. I remember how you helped my mother, how you've come to my defense on more than one occasion in spite of the bad blood between our families."

She paused in front of him, looking up into light brown eyes for any remnant of the compassion he'd shown her in the past. She was disappointed.

17

"That was many years ago, Lynn. If you came here in the hopes of finding the boy in the man you are sadly mistaken."

"Obviously I am, I thought you were better than Tom Rangell," she muttered under her breath before turning to leave. *Logan warned her about turning to Jake for help, she should have listened.*

Lynn gasped as her arm was grabbed roughly. Jake whipped her around with a force that had her neck snapping at the jarring motion.

"What did you say?" The anger she'd glimpsed earlier was alive in full force now.

"I didn't mean—"

"I know exactly what you meant. You know, I think I've had a change of heart."

"You have?" she stammered, both arms in his hold now. The harsh veil that fell over his face didn't bode well.

He nodded. "I would be willing to loan the equipment for your little venture with your brothers," he said sweetly, a little too sweetly for her liking.

"You would?" She hesitated as his almost painful grip refused to relax.

"That is, if you're willing to pay the price."

"Um…I'm sure I can work something out with our budget." Warning bells sounded in the back of her mind, with renewed hope she ignored them.

"I'm not talking about monetary compensation."

"You're not?"

He shook his head slowly.

"Then what?" It came out in a croak as his face inched closer to her own. Teenage fantasies came to her in a rush of unrequited desires. How many hours had she spent daydreaming about this man in her youth? She'd dedicated notebooks full of poems and stories to him. Now, they were both adults, and as much as she hated to admit it to herself she still found him as appealing as ever, even in his current state of anger.

"Do you think you're ready to pay the ultimate price for your family?"

At her wide-eyed silence he continued.

"Agree to stay with me for two weeks."

"Stay…here…with you? Why?"

"Why else, Lynn? Tell me, are you willing to trade this delectably lush body of yours to save your family's ranch?"

Maybe his proximity dulled her senses, or was it that he continued to hold her so tightly? Whatever the reason, it took her a moment to digest his meaning.

"How dare you!" she spat, trying unsuccessfully to jerk one arm free. Her palm itched to connect with his arrogant face.

"Would you like to see just how much I dare? You remember the kissing booth at the county fair all those years ago? You were barely legal but everything about you screamed woman. Remember how our kiss went?"

Did she ever, it had been her first real kiss. Her line had been long, filled with teenage boys from the two local high schools. Her brothers chased a majority of them off over the years whenever one got bold enough to ask her on a date. They saw this as their only opportunity to sample the goods. She'd just started packing up to change shifts with a friend when Jake appeared.

"Leaving so soon?"

Her heart had pounded in her chest at the familiar voice.

"Jake?"

"In the flesh and with a ticket," he handed her the orange stub.

"Um...okay."

She had leaned over the narrow expanse of the booth to give him the customary peck.

"Not like that," he had whispered before pulling her as close as the barrier would allow and swooping down to capture her full lips.

* * * *

"You wouldn't," she whispered. The memory of their kiss wreaked havoc on her blood pressure.

In answer his head dipped further to close the gap between them. The first contact of flesh on flesh sent her heart soaring. Jake forced her mouth open with his own, demanding full access, and for all her protesting she let him in with minimal resistance.

Lynn's reeling mind vaguely logged her hands being trapped between their bodies while his arms snaked around her. One pulled her closer by the waist, the other dropped to allow his hand bold access to her denim clad derriere.

"You've always had the nicest ass in Garrett County," he muttered against her lips.

His words effectively grounded her like a douse of cold water.

"Let me go." She tried in vain to wiggle free.

"And if I don't?"

With as much strength as she could muster, she drew her knee up straight for the obvious arousal pushing into her pelvic bone. He deflected the swift assault with his hard thigh, causing Lynn to yelp.

"I would advise against that in the future, sweetling."

"Don't call me that," she said with venom, hating that he was able to avoid injury and still keep her secured in his arms. *Stupid self-defense classes weren't worth crap.*

Just as quickly as she'd been grabbed Jake let her go, and she stumbled away from him and into the foyer in angry silence.

"I'll give you a day to think on my proposal, Lynn. If I don't hear from you, I'll assume you've come up with an alternative solution."

* * * *

Jake wasn't certain he'd heard right when his housekeeper announced who was waiting for him in the foyer. Lynn James, he hadn't heard her name in over eleven years, although he'd be lying to himself if he said his thoughts hadn't strayed in her direction several times over that period. Recently, images of her plagued him more than he cared to acknowledge, which was why he'd avoided any contact with her since her return six months ago—a small feat given the proximity of their ranches.

Time had been a generous friend to her. Lynn had grown beautifully into her womanly curves, as he'd known she would. She'd always been a tall, thick woman, the perfect size for someone of his height and stature, with all the right proportions for a man to appreciate. Her oval-shaped face showcased

21

lush, kissable lips, narrow nose, and almond shaped eyes so dark they could barely be called brown. She'd worn her hair pulled back in a ponytail making her look younger than her thirty years.

He was proud of himself for not standing there and gawking like some love-struck adolescent, although his body's reaction to her was instantaneous. He definitely needed the short walk to his office to calm his riotous nerves. Good lord, he was pushing forty, far too old for such a pubescent response, especially when it seemed so obvious that she wasn't there for a social visit.

Jake was correct in his quick assumption that her impromptu arrival had to do with the land he'd acquired from her stepbrothers. He pushed back the disappointment, reminding himself that there was no reason for him to expect any other reason for her sudden appearance. He'd never made his feelings for her known. Well, other than the brief kiss at the fair those many years ago, but she'd practically high-tailed it straight for the Harringtons' no sooner than the encounter ended. It was obvious from her response that she didn't share his attraction. He'd felt like an old pervert lusting after a girl not fully out of her teens.

Part of him wondered if it would forever be the curse of Rangell men to hanker after James women. His father had spent a lifetime loving a woman who detested him. Jake watched how that love turned Tom into a bitter, mean spirited man. Admittedly, he'd even felt a certain amount of animosity towards Kathleen James-Harrington for remaining in Garrett County and marrying their closest neighbor. He knew his anger was misplaced and felt his fair share of guilt in his adult years for it, but the teenaged Jake lived with the repercussions of his father's yearning.

His mother, a once very loving woman, turned into a temperamental harpy over night. She'd ostracized anything male, especially with the Rangell name attached to it, including her own son. Instead of leaving her husband of nineteen years she vowed instead to make his life a living hell. Unfortunately, her anger wound up hitting Jake all too often. Her loathing for his father slowly ate away at her like the cancer that would eventually claim her life. It was ironic that the tragedy that tore their family apart pushed father and son closer together, forging a bond between them that until this day Jake didn't fully understand.

Seeing Lynn again brought all the memories to the present, reminding Jake of a history he'd hoped to not revisit. When she sat across from him, all high and mighty accusing him of unfair business practices, he bit back a sarcastic response that would have revealed the truth of how he'd acquired their lands. He now regretted that he hadn't been able to hold a check on his temper at the comparison to his father. Mixed emotions prompted his response, a part of him wanting her to see just how much like Tom Rangell he could be by making the absurd request. If he hadn't been holding her, he was certain she would have bolted like a skittish doe.

He felt a small satisfaction in seeing her stumble away from him with disbelieving eyes. Good, his mission had been accomplished. Lynn James would never darken his doorstep again. With any luck she would eventually return to Arizona and not doom him to a similar torture his father endured: knowing the woman he wanted was only a short distance away but unable to reach out for her.

* * * *

"So?" Ryan, her eldest brother, was on her as soon as she walked through the front door.

"Damn!" She clutched her chest at her rapidly beating heart that had already been in over drive since Jake's kiss. "Can you not sneak up on a girl like that?"

"Sorry. So, what happened?"

"Where's Logan?" she wanted to know.

"He's out at the site. Now quit stalling and tell me what happened."

"Two-way Logan. We'll talk about it as a family."

Ryan huffed his displeasure at being dismissed, but went in search of the two-way.

Lynn couldn't really give a rat's ass about Ryan's feelings on the topic. If it weren't for his rashness and loose purse strings they wouldn't need to have the dreaded conversation. More good looks and selfishness than brains, Ryan had single-handedly dwindled what should have been a fortune down to virtually nothing, forcing him and Logan to sell cattle and land off to Jake Rangell—unbeknownst to their aging father. Logan, content to handle the day-to-day activities, had unwittingly left the finances to his older brother without question. It wasn't until supplies stopped coming in with regularity that he'd confronted Ryan and learned the reality of their situation. Neither thought to seek her help, When she lived in Arizona, where she worked as a CPA. When Logan finally tossed pride aside and phoned up "Twittle" — the nickname she'd been coined with as a child — they were so far in the red Lynn didn't think she could do anything to help.

"Have you told Daddy?" she'd asked after hearing the whole story.

"No, he doesn't know about any of it yet," Logan had admitted. Lynn recalled how he'd sounded so tired and lost.

"I'll fly out this weekend, tell Ryan to have everything ready for me to go over."

That had been six months ago, and she'd invested her life savings and the proceeds from the sale of her condo into the ranch. The Harrington had originally been a cattle ranch, but with the mismanagement of funds, their father's illness, and the inability to pay ranch hands, it turned into a laughing stock. For months after her arrival Logan and Lynn pored over finances and brainstormed while they struggled to get creditors off their backs and keep the meager work crew on board.

Logan confided in his younger sibling one night that he believed there was oil in the eastern region of the ranch. He'd done his own soil samples and had them verified by a local geologist, who'd confirmed his hopes. They'd both agreed that the capital from even a couple of oil wells was enough to put The Harrington back in business as a fully functioning cattle ranch. Lynn spent tireless hours going over expenditures, bills and necessities until she came up with a working budget to keep them afloat and invest in their drilling venture.

"You've got to be kidding if you expect me to live on this," Ryan had complained.

"You can either live on it or go get a job," she replied as she presented her plan to her brothers .

"Now listen here, Twittle, you can't just come in here and start dictating things 'cause you gave us a little bit of money," he continued, trying to mask his anger.

"Shut up, Ryan. I'm so fed up with you and your shit right now I could kick your ass from here to Austin," Logan responded in irritation. It wasn't the last time Ryan would grumble about the new way things were being ran, but he'd made sure to complain to Lynn when Logan wasn't around.

* * * *

"That's it then." Ryan bowed his head, shoulder's slumped as if the enormity of everything had finally weighed them down completely.

"No, we still have a few other avenues we could pursue," Lynn said as they sat discussing her earlier meeting with Jake. She chose to omit his final offer.

"Lynn, we've tried all of our contacts here in Texas. As much as I hate to admit it, I think Ryan is right. We should tell Paw." Logan ran a frustrated hand through his sandy blond hair.

"No," Lynn shook her head. "We can't put him through that now, he needs to focus on getting well."

"I don't know. I think we need to prepare him for the inevitable. You've put forth a good effort, and because of you we won't come out of this in debt. I promise you we will give all of your money back."

"Hey wait a second. Dad invested a lot in her fancy educations. I don't think—" Ryan surfaced from his stupor to rant.

"Shut up, Ryan," Logan sighed, the defeat in his voice striking a cord with her.

"Don't worry I'll come up with something, we're not going to lose The Harrington," she promised.

Two

The late Texas morning air was cool and calm, too calm. Even the birds that normally chirped their morning sonnets seemed to wait with baited breath, as if knowing the monumental task that lay ahead of her. Lynn wasn't sure how long she sat in Jake's driveway trying to gain the courage to walk up to his front door and knock. So deep in thought was she that the buzzing of her cell phone had her jumping in her seat.

She stared unblinkingly at the Caller ID before answering.

"How long do you plan to sit out there?" Jake's gruff voice asked over the phone.

"How did you...? I dropped some papers that I'm trying to gather."

"Uh huh, well, gather your courage quickly. I have a ranch to run." He clicked off, sounding irritated. How dare he sound annoyed when she was about to do the unthinkable?

"Asshole," she muttered.

* * * *

"Mr. Rangell will be with you shortly," his personal assistant informed as he escorted her into Jake's office.

Of course he would stretch this out by keeping me waiting even longer, she thought, shifting restlessly in the chair she'd taken. Of all the controlling things to do. He knew what her answer was, had known when she called him that morning to tell him of her decision, only to have him interrupt and order her back out to his ranch to discuss it face to face.

"I hope you were able to rescue your...papers," Jake greeted her, coming into the room and closing the door securely behind him.

"Um...yes."

"Good, so why don't we get down to business?" Instead of taking a seat behind his desk like before, he propped himself on its edge in front of her. He looked casually sexy in another pair of faded jeans, this time with a gray T-shirt. From her vantage point in the soft leather chair, she could see the very prominent bulge in his pants. The denim stretched invitingly across his hefty swell and Lynn made every effort to avert her eyes.

Not wanting to think about the thickness that lay beneath the material, she began, "I've had a chance to consider your offer and, under the circumstances, think that I can live with the arrangement."

He nodded his acknowledgement.

"And have you discussed this with your family?"

"No," she answered quickly. "They don't know."

"So you just plan to disappear for two weeks?"

"No, actually, I was hoping that maybe we could make a modification to your request."

"What kind of modification?"

"Well, we could spend a couple of days together at a time to avoid anyone knowing," she suggested.

"No, Lynn. It's two weeks on Rangell Ranch with me, or nothing at all. If you're worried about offending your family's sensibilities, perhaps you should look for another option."

"I told you there aren't other alternatives in Texas, and we can't afford to go out of state."

He shrugged. "As I said earlier I have a ranch to run, so what's it to be?"

"Yes," she mumbled under her breath.

"I'm sorry, I didn't catch that." He cocked his head as if to hear better.

"I said yes, damn you. I agree to your terms."

Lynn thought she noticed a slight hesitation before Jake responded.

"Good. I've arranged to have the equipment delivered tomorrow morning at seven, I'll be by at that time to collect you."

Collect me, like I'm some sort of object, she silently fumed.

"That's not necessary, I can drive myself."

"I insist."

"All right." She would have protested further, but didn't see the point her fate was sealed, at least for two weeks. "Then I guess I should get back and prepare Logan for the equipment."

"Not so fast." He rose with her, reaching out to pull her easily in his arms.

"What are you doing?" she asked, a little too breathlessly.

"Sealing the deal."

This time his kiss was slow, lips moving over hers gently until she opened to him fully. He dug a hand in her short bobbed hair, his kiss going from gentle to possessive domination in a matter of seconds.

"Wrap your arms around my neck," he mumbled against her mouth. When she hesitated, he growled, "Do it." He punctuated the command with a firm swat to her backside.

This time she complied, not wanting to admit just how exciting she found his method of persuasion.

"You will do whatever I ask, whenever I ask it. Is that understood?" He moved his lips to trail her neck.

She nodded.

"Answer me."

"Yes."

"Good girl, now run along home and prepare yourself for me," he said, setting her away from him.

* * * *

He should feel like a heel. Should feel like a complete rat for even contemplating going forward with what had only been an off the cuff proposal made in anger. When Lynn called him that morning to agree to his outlandish request, he was floored, literally rendered speechless for several seconds. He'd found his voice amidst her nervous speech. She couldn't be serious, which was why he'd insisted she come to Rangell Ranch to talk further. He was certain she would be a no-show. He knew, before their brief conversation ended, that he would help her without her agreeing to his demand.

31

In the time it took her to drive to the ranch, Jake had it all worked out. He would have the equipment loaded that day and delivered the following morning. He'd inform her that there was no reason to go forward with his proposition. Assuring her that the financial compensation she'd outlined earlier would more than suffice. That was his intention, until he saw her and the thought was immediately replaced by the desire to taste her again. How did the expression go, the road to hell is paved with good intentions? Heaven help him. If she hadn't felt so good in his arms, yielded so easily to his touch, he could have contented himself with the brief encounter and remembered his plan.

Nothing was written in stone, he appeased himself. There was always tomorrow, yes a perfect day for redemption.

* * * *

"Hell no!" Logan roared as she explained the situation that evening after dinner, bounding from the porch swing he'd sat in seconds earlier. They were alone now since Ryan left to meet one of his many girlfriends, while Race retired early. This had left Lynn and Logan to drift outside on the porch to enjoy the quiet, star-filled night. Regardless of the heat, she loved Texas in the summer, and it was one of those perfectly warm nights, just right for sitting out.

"Listen to me," she pleaded.

"There's nothing to hear, I will not let you prostitute yourself."

Lynn closed her eyes against his harsh words. She'd tried to look at her arrangement with Jake from many angles, but found herself coming back to the same conclusion as her brother. Ultimately, she would be trading her body for profit, and the fact she was doing so with Jake Rangell was bittersweet. Over the years she tried not to let the images of Jake dominate her thoughts. Years of longing left her with a curiosity only he could satisfy.

"Your mother would roll over in her grave if she knew what you were suggesting," he continued.

"You're making it sound worse than it is. You of all people know how much of a crush I had on Jake growing up. It's not like I haven't thought about it." *And dreamed about it*, she added silently.

"Puppy love," he dismissed. "We're adults now, Lynn."

"Exactly, with adult sized problems. It's our only solution, lets face it, Logan, no one is going to come to our rescue."

"Hell, we'll come up with another one." He bound from the swing to pace the length of the porch.

"Don't you think I've looked at this from every angle? I'm okay, really."

"I can't believe what I'm hearing."

"Believe it, 'cause I've already made up my mind. I need your help in making sure Daddy doesn't get wind of this."

"Talk about causing him another stroke," he huffed.

"That's why he can't know. I'd hoped to have you and Ryan here together, but knowing him he won't be back until tomorrow afternoon so you'll need to bring him up to speed."

Logan's pacing ended abruptly, leaving him to lean against the wooden railing as if he needed the extra support. Lynn took in his profile while he stared out into the still of the night. The wheels turning in his head were almost noticeable as he tried to come up with another option. She silently observed, knowing his train of thought was probably venturing down the same track her own had traveled over the last day. Finally he cursed aloud, hanging and shaking his head in refusal of the undeniable conclusion she'd already arrived at.

"Logan?" When he didn't answer she moved behind him, wrapping arms around his waist. She rested her cheek against his solid back.

"I can do this, I need to do this." When he still didn't answer, she added, "It's the only way."

"Yeah, but it doesn't mean I have to like it." His tone was barely audible, but she'd heard him and knew that was the closest thing to an agreement she would get.

* * * *

"Well, land sakes, what's all this?" Race asked, propelling his electric wheel chair towards the bay window, staring out at the procession of trucks coming through the entrance of The Harrington.

"It's equipment, Daddy," Lynn answered, trying to will away the nervous energy building inside her.

"I can see that. What in God's name is it for?"

"For oil drilling, remember?"

"Ah yes, Logan's big idea." He nodded.

Lynn was happy to see him looking less pale that morning. She didn't think she'd ever get use to the shell of a man his stroke had left behind.

34

"I need to get going. My ride will be here any minute to take me to the airport."

"Yes, of course. If your other, good for nothing brother were around he could take you instead of Jake Rangell," he snorted disapprovingly.

Normally Lynn would have come to Ryan's rescue, like she'd done whenever Race began his put downs, but she thought it better not to get into an argument with him at the moment. The fact that he hadn't questioned her more about getting a ride from Jake was a blessing in disguise. She'd prepared herself for a barrage of questions that never came. She doubted Logan would be so lucky later on, and hoped he could stand up to their father's interrogation.

"Daddy, Jake volunteered and I didn't see any reason not to take him up on his offer since he's always been nice to me," the lie slipped easily from her lips. "Remember, I'll be gone for two weeks, but if you need anything just call me on my cell phone and I'll get the first flight out of Arizona."

"Don't worry, the boys are here, you just hurry up back. I'm so glad you decided to come home, Twittle."

"Me too, Daddy." She leaned over to brush a loving kiss against his forehead, grateful at how easily he'd accepted her cover story.

"I gotta go." Lynn hurried as she saw Jake's black long bed pull into the circular drive. He eased out of the truck's dual cab, his attention caught by something that obviously didn't meet his approval from the scowl on his face.

"Have a safe trip," Race's frail voice called after as she rushed into the warming morning air.

She paused in the doorway when she realized Logan was the distraction that had Jake glowering. There was definitely no love lost between the two men, but Lynn suspected their beef with each other went beyond their parents' issues.

The men stood only a few feet apart, but were engaged in a conversation audible only to them. Jake's eyes immediately landed on her seconds before Logan looked over his shoulder to see his sister step onto the front porch. Jake uttered something else not meant for her ears, causing her brother to turn back on their guest angrily.

"Jake, would you mind helping me with these bags?" Lynn interrupted what looked to be a heated retort.

"Sure." He gave Logan one long look before coming to the porch to grab both her cases.

"Logan," she repeated his name twice when it looked as if he would stop the other man. She bounded down the stairs to hook her arm through her stepbrother's.

"You don't have to do this, Lynn," he repeated, as he'd done many times since last night. He shifted them to effectively block Jake and his pickup from view. The worried look in his eyes touched her.

"We've been through this, Logan," she whispered.

"Lynn, it's time to go," Jake called as he completed his task.

Lynn looked around her brother's broad shoulder to see Jake heading back in their direction instead of waiting in the truck like she'd hoped. The permanent grimace on his face made it clear that he was annoyed.

"Stay, and we'll find another solution," Logan almost pleaded.

"We don't have time, we need to start drilling soon." She glanced between the two men, not liking the determined look on Jake's face. "I'll call you," she promised, standing on tiptoes to brush a kiss on his cheek before stepping around him to intercept Jake, who didn't seem content to stand idly by.

In Jake's path, she squared her shoulders. "I'm ready."

"Glad to hear it." He gave one hard look over her head before gently propelling her towards the waiting truck.

Lynn could feel the tension in the air as Jake closed the passenger door. For several moments the men held each other's gaze, and she found herself wringing her hands with anticipation. When Logan finally gave a final look in her direction she furnished him with her best reassuring smile.

"You realize he's in love with you." They'd just pulled out of the main entrance of The Harrington when Jake finally spoke.

"Of course he loves me, he's my brother." She focused her gaze on the familiar scenery, noting how rapidly the place she'd called home for many years shrank away.

"That's not what I mean."

It took a moment for his words to sink in, but when they did she whipped around in outrage.

"You're sick. Logan and Ryan have thought of me as their sister from the moment I stepped foot on The Harrington."

"Perhaps, at one time." The taut set of his jaw served to only add to her frustration with him.

Determined not to give further credence to his ludicrous utterance, she continued her vigil on the passing landscape. Flat lands stretched as far as the eye could see between The Harrington and Rangell Ranch spreads. An outcropping of trees littered the open range in a sporadic assembly, allowing cattle to seek reprieve under their shading, while others grazed lazily in pastures, not sparing the passing vehicle the briefest of glances. It was a good twenty-minute drive between the Rangell and Harrington spreads, and she didn't care if Jake didn't say another word to her in that entire period.

By the time Rangell Ranch came into view Lynn had never been happier to see the place. At least there she could temporarily escape Jake and his lewd suggestions. To think that her own brother could harbor such feelings for her was absurd.

"Take these up to my room," Logan ordered Chris, his assistant. As he greeted them.

The younger man looked between Jake and the woman, before taking the cases from his employer to comply with the request.

"You could have been more subtle," Lynn admonished when she was certain they were alone.

"What for? Chris is here everyday, as well as other members of my staff. I think it will be fairly obvious to all of them the nature of our relationship."

"Temporary arrangement," she corrected, twirling in time to see him head back over the threshold to the front porch.

"Whatever. I have a lot of things to see to this morning and afternoon. I should be back in time for dinner."

"You're leaving? Well you could have just left me at The Harrington until you were done with your work. I'm sure Logan could use my help," she snapped, not quite sure why she was so upset when she should have felt relief at the temporary reprieve.

"I think you've done enough for him at the moment, but if you'd much prefer we begin the nature of our *arrangement* now, I'm willing to play hooky today."

Lynn gasped when he unexpectedly closed the gap between them, leaving her no opportunity to retreat into the recesses of the foyer.

"Is that what you want, sweetling? Do you want to stay here with me?" He gathered her in his arms, bending until only a breath separated them. "Are you so eager for my touch that you can't wait until tonight?"

She didn't have a chance to respond before his lips captured hers in a kiss that was meant to arouse and possess. She wasn't going to give in this time, she told herself. She wanted him to know that he couldn't control her responses. She did well, at first, until her traitorous body gave up the short battle. She whimpered when he abruptly pulled away, only to find herself cradled easily in his arms as if she weighed nothing more than a few pounds. His strides were quick and purposeful as he made his way to the stairs.

"Sorry," Chris apologized immediately when they nearly collided with the forgotten man at the bottom of the stairs.

The heat that crept up her neck took up residence in her cheeks and threatened to consume her entire body.

"Um...should I instruct the men this morning?" The embarrassment on the young man's face almost rivaled her own as he backed up two steps to give them space.

"No," Lynn answered at the same moment Jake was saying yes. The red-faced man turned a darker shade. He found a sudden interest in his feet, quickly averting his gaze.

"Put me down," Lynn ordered softly. "Please," she added when it looked as if Jake would ignore her request.

Grudgingly, he placed her on the step above him, which still left her a few inches shorter than his towering frame. A protective arm encircled her waist, bringing him in very intimate proximity with her backside.

"Wait for me in the truck," he instructed the other man, who seemed to be waiting for the pardon because he made quick work of maneuvering around the couple and out the front door.

Lynn waited for Jake's next move, certain now that she was safe from a continuation of his manhandling.

She could feel his warm breath on her neck; the heat teased her bare skin. She was amazed how excitedly her body responded to his nearness. Never had a man stirred her desires so easily.

"We'll finish this later," he vowed.

She sagged against the banister in relief when she heard the front door closing in his wake, realizing that she'd been holding her breath until that moment. What the hell was it about this man that had her body going haywire? How in God's name was she going to endure the next two weeks without loosing herself to him?

* * * *

Jake inhaled deeply on the porch, trying to get his hormones under control. He hadn't intended for things to go this far. He had planned to drop the equipment at The Harrington and return home to see to his day's work, alone. Instead he'd been unable to tear his eyes away from the beautiful, dark-skinned woman as she exited her family's home in jeans that looked like a second skin on her thick frame. Her yellow T-shirt stretched across full breasts, molding the lush mounds. Logan, who'd been lying in wait for him, turned at his sudden silence and Jake immediately recognized the unrequited attraction evident in the younger man's gaze as he took in her womanly curves in a non-brotherly fashion.

"Put your eyes back in your head, Harrington," he'd said for the younger man's ears only.

"Listen, Rangell, you hurt one hair on her head and so help me…" The threat came after the man waved to the approaching woman.

"You'll what, Harrington?"

Lynn interrupted them at that moment, but Jake didn't need a response to know what was on Logan

Harrington's mind. It was a thought that he'd shared and expressed on more than one occasion, both of which involved Lynn James. Neither man wanted harm to come to her and would cause injury to anyone stupid enough to try.

Coming up, Jake purposefully kept a wide birth of the budding woman, but as Lynn grew into womanhood so did his attraction to her. Their family feud and age difference kept him from seeing her the way he'd wanted, but fate always seemed to throw the two together. He was there the day she and some friends hung out at the town ice cream parlor and overheard a group of white teenaged boys debating over who would be the first to "nail the little black girl." He'd promptly put an end to the discussion with a warning of very descriptive bodily harm should anyone lay a hand on her. After the kissing booth incident she seemed to plague his mind to distraction, so much so that his father commented on it during an outing where they spotted Lynn shopping with her mother.

"I see you've fallen victim to the love bug yourself," the elder Rangell said after catching a distracted Jake watching the girl slip into a local boutique. He'd heard that Lynn was home for the summer after her freshman year of college. Unfortunately for him, he spied her with his father and her mother in tow.

"What are you talking about, Paw?"

"Don't try to pretend like you weren't looking at Kathleen's little girl. I know you've had a thing for her for years."

"You don't know what you're saying. I'm almost ten years her senior."

"In my day something like age wouldn't have mattered much."

"Well, it matters to me."

"Maybe one day it won't." The older man's gaze hung on the door that closed behind daughter and mother. If the situation hadn't been so pathetic Jake would have laughed out loud. What a pair the two men made, lusting after women who ignored their very existence.

When Lynn showed up at his doorstep two days ago, he was certain he was over his infatuation, only to find that it had lain dormant for all the years of her absence. Seeing her for the first time in eleven years threw him for a complete loop. He found himself wanting to know what she'd been doing with herself. Was there anyone serious in her life? How long she would be staying? Obviously, she was still unmarried, leaving him to wonder if the men in Arizona were blind or just stupid. Instead of catching up on the many missing years, she'd launched into her accusation followed by the "business proposal," which promptly put him in his place and made the nature of their future relationship clear.

At any point he could have set her straight and informed her about how Ryan sought him out to sell a portion of The Harrington. How he would have sold more for mere pennies if Jake had agreed. How would she feel to learn that he had no intention of doing anything with the land and livestock except return it to the family once they'd rectified their financial woes?

When Jake suggested she exchange herself for the equipment necessary to save their ranch he'd done so in anger, was certain that Lynn would give him a big piece of her mind and walk away without a backwards glance. He was wrong, which only illustrated the extent of her desperation. His hands clenched into a fist at the thought of her agreeing to the same sort of arrangement with anyone else.

Now he stood at the precipice of a major decision: walk right back in his home and absolve her, or continue with the outrageous arrangement. When faced with the thought of letting her return to The Harrington where Logan would greet her with open arms his choice was clear.

Three

Lynn paced the entire Rangell home several times over, more to release some pent up energy than to get reacquainted with the lay of the house. Although she hadn't been inside since her mother had worked there, she remembered every nook and cranny as if she'd never left. She visited some of her favorite childhood hiding spaces where she would quietly observe her mother, unbeknownst to the busy woman. In spite of how things ended, she'd had a happy childhood roaming freely in the wide expanse. By comparison, the Rangell home was twice the size of the Harringtons', and Lynn wondered if at one point the plan was to fill its eight bedrooms with children.

She wandered upstairs to the room she knew Jake occupied growing up, wondering if he'd remained in the sanctuary of his youth. Her hunch was correct. Although he hadn't bothered to take up residence in the master bedroom, he had taken the liberty of knocking down the connecting wall between the bedrooms on either side of his own to make, himself a veritable suite. The room was done in deep, cherry wood and dark greens, colors that reminded her of Jake's overpowering masculinity. Lynn couldn't help but wonder if a girlfriend or designer was responsible for the coordinated ensemble of furniture and accessories.

She didn't leave a piece untouched in her exploration, and while she initially ignored his bed it was obviously the focal point of the room. Sitting smack dab in its center, its high four post looked like towers, as they seemed to reach for the vaulted ceilings. Lynn could picture Jake lying in the raised bed, sleeping soundly between the rich sheets. A rush of heat blanketed her body as she thought of the two of them together in it, a contortion of legs and arms.

"God give me strength," she muttered before remembering her reason for being in the room in the first place. She easily located her two cases and headed for his closet to hang her meager belongings, deciding to keep her more intimate apparel in one case. Considering what she'd agreed to do for the next two weeks, she knew it was probably silly to be uncomfortable with the idea of her personal things mingling with his, but there was nothing normal about their short-term living arrangement.

As was typical on a ranch, Lynn didn't expect Jake back until after sunset, which seemed a lifetime away. With nothing left to do she debated calling Logan but thought better of it. He had a ton of work ahead of him and didn't need to be distracted by her. Instead, she made her way to the kitchen as an idea came to mind. Hopefully Jake's housekeeper hadn't started on the evening meal. If the woman was anything like her mother, she would prepare the meal hours ahead of time just in case her employer decided to dine early, or in case her chores took longer than she'd anticipated.

She briefly made the woman's acquaintance that afternoon after she found Lynn investigating the library. The housekeeper wasn't surprised by her presence, which led her to believe she'd already been briefed about the temporary houseguest. The thin, middle-aged woman introduced herself as Helen, informing Lynn that she usually worked five days a week from noon until six unless otherwise requested by Mr. Rangell, and that she would be available should Lynn need anything. Helen seemed nice enough, but it was obvious that she wouldn't be much company for her during those long days. It would be a painstakingly slow two weeks if she didn't find something to occupy her time.

"It looks like you have everything taken care of in here, so I think I'll be leaving now," Helen said sometime later as she came back into the kitchen. She eyed the several pots on the stove approvingly.

"Okay, and thanks for showing me where everything was in here."

"No problem. Just leave the dishes. I'll take care of them tomorrow," were her parting words. Once again Lynn was alone in the house.

The aroma of spices, vegetables and meat mingled in the kitchen like a delightful promise. Maybe she'd overdone things just a bit, Lynn surmised as she first stirred the heaping pot of greens, then the candied yams marinating on the stovetop. Steaks, macaroni casserole, and dinner rolls stayed warm in the oven. She'd made enough to feed them for breakfast, lunch, and dinner over the next couple days, if they weren't joined by some of the ranch hands, which was a possibility. She wondered if there was enough time to get an apple pie going, but thought better of it. Their arrangement was strictly for business purposes, at least on her part, she silently reassured.

Why Jake insisted on this arrangement in the first place was beyond her. It wasn't like he couldn't get a woman with a simple crook of a finger. As far back as she could remember women were always on steady supply to him. Hell, she was surprised to find he was still unmarried. She'd expected to find him permanently attached to one of the beautiful, down home girls she'd seen on his arm on several occasions in her youth, complete with a passel of little Rangells underfoot.

She stiffened, pondering his reasoning. Maybe he'd always been curious about black women, and this was his way of living out some jungle fever fantasy. She dismissed the thought easily. There were enough attractive sisters in their town now who would give Jake the time of day without a second thought. Which brought her back to her initial question, why her?

* * * *

"Something smells good in here." The sudden appearance of the man who'd preoccupied her mind all day now had her heart in her throat. She'd just stepped out of the pantry when he suddenly materialized.

"I was bored," she replied as he took in the buffet laid out on the center granite island. "I thought maybe some of your men would be joining us."

Jake's gaze pinned her to the spot. "Not tonight."

He looked like a man who'd put in an honest days work, from his dusty work boots and jeans, stained shirt, stubble shadowed face, and mused hair. *Damn, he looks good*, she thought, lowering her gaze.

"I'll go upstairs and freshen up, and we can have dinner in here."

"Oh, I thought maybe the formal dinning room—"

"Right here, we've been separated long enough today. The last thing I want is to put that behemoth of a table between us."

Lynn stood in the same spot for several moments after Jake left the room. She wasn't surprised to find the towel in her hand twisted into a taut line, because that's exactly how she felt, all twisted and wound just as tight as the cloth whenever he was around.

Time ticked by slowly while she waited for his return. She contemplated setting the dining room table just to be ornery but thought better of it. As much as she hated to admit it, Jake called the shots.

What was taking him so long, she wondered, but answered her own question as the image of him showering away the day's grime came rushing to the forefront of her mind. "What is my problem?" Lynn muttered. "He's just a man." She busied herself loading food onto both their plates as a distraction, humming her favorite Jaguar Wright song.

"You've outdone yourself."

Okay, she was definitely going to get him a bell, Lynn decided as he startled her for a second time.

"There wasn't much else for me to do today," she answered, moving to take a seat, unwilling to make eye contact with him.

"I seem to remember offering to stay at home." He sat opposite her, long legs stretching underneath the table and connecting with her own. The position wasn't accidental, she knew as he trapped one of her legs.

She ignored his response as she dug into her meal with pretend relish, wishing she'd had the foresight to tuck her legs under her. In reality if someone had asked her what the food tasted like that evening, Lynn was certain she wouldn't be able to answer honestly since her total focus was now on ignoring the man across from her. His fresh scent combining with the flavorful food aromas was an enticement all its own. Her heart rate accelerated with every breath.

"This is delicious, but you didn't have to cook," he broke the silence.

"I didn't mind."

"I remember your mother's food tasting this way."

That got a response. Her eyes met honeyed ones.

"You remember her cooking?

"Yes, anyone else Dad hired could never get it quite right."

"I don't think anyone's cooking could ever come close to Mom's, not even mine. And I was right there helping with every meal."

"Well, you've come very close, she would be proud," he said between bites.

Logan's earlier comment came to mind, and Lynn wasn't certain how proud her mother would be to see her in her current state.

"One thing I've never perfected is her meat loaf," she admitted as a way to change the direction of her thoughts.

"Hmmm, I'd like to be the judge of that," he offered.

"All right," she agreed.

"You keep this up and I might not be willing to let you go after two weeks."

Her mouth went dry as she tried to swallow her last bite. *Get a grip girl, he's only joking. It's obvious Jake is the poster boy for bachelorhood. Besides, you have your life to get back to once this is over.*

The remainder of the meal was eaten in near silence, with him polishing off another plate of food before calling it quits. Despite Helen's request Lynn emptied the leftovers in containers, scrubbed the pots and pans, and loaded the dishwasher with Jake at her side. He'd brushed up against her so often she was beginning to think he was doing it on purpose.

"What are you doing?" Lynn gasped as she found herself trapped between him and the counter. He braced hands on either side of her, making it impossible for escape. She could push against his chest but doubted that would do anything but afford her a free feel of his hard chest. Not a bad thought, but she needed to keep things in perspective.

"I've wanted to do this all day," he whispered before capturing her lips between his own. The first contact sent her mind reeling. Jake teased her mouth with his plundering tongue.

"Are you protected?" he asked, pulling away halfheartedly.

"Protected?" Yeah she felt pretty secure, and very aroused.

"Birth control," he clarified.

"Um...yes...I use the patch," she supplied, nervously pointing to an area on her upper arm.

He nodded his understanding, "Good, because when I take you tonight I don't want there to be any barriers between us."

She felt herself growing moist at the thought of him bare inside her.

"As far as everything else I'm healthy," he volunteered.

She nodded. "Me, too." Hell, this would be her first experience being with a man without the protection of a condom. Despite the circumstances, a part of her was happy to share such an intimate encounter with him.

"Go upstairs and change into a robe, nothing else, and meet me in the hot tub. If you didn't bring one mine is on the back of the bathroom door." He dropped one arm, seeming to fully expect her compliance.

"I don't think—"

"Good, don't. I will have your complete submission, Lynn, for the next two weeks. I won't have it any other way."

Her next objection died on her lips at the severe look he gave her.

"Ten minutes," he called after her retreating form.

* * * *

"Complete submission," she mumbled in his room as she yanked jeans down over her rounded hips. Her blouse followed next with equal force. Soon her bra and panties met the same fate. "I'll tell you what you can do with your ten minutes."

Depositing her clothes in the hamper, she caught a glimpse of her naked frame in the bathroom mirror and paused. Good lord! What was she thinking? One look at her and Jake was sure to think he'd been cheated. Granted, she'd never been a thin girl, but as a woman her curves were definitely fuller, thighs thicker. She stared at her naked reflection, dissecting each body part. Obsession with being skinny wasn't a weakness of hers like some full figured women. She'd accepted long ago that it just wasn't in the cards for her to be petite. Until that moment she'd never given it much thought. Hell, she'd never had a shortage of dates during or after college. Overall, her self image was positive, but somehow she just didn't see Jake appreciating her ample proportions.

"Take it or leave it," she said to her reflection.

Luckily she didn't need Jake's massive robe, having come prepared with her own. She slipped into the soft white silk of her favorite garment, belting it at the waist. It was purchased on a whim while shopping in her favorite boutique, after Lynn found that nothing else would do. Although tightly secured the front dipped into a deep vee, the robe exposed a generous view of her neck and the swell of her cleavage. It stopped just above her ankles, swishing around shapely legs as she walked barefoot to her fate.

* * * *

Jake positioned himself to see the exact moment she emerged through the sliding glass doors. Around him the hot tub bubbled in full force, the water nicely heated, or was it him?

Lynn looked every bit the regal, full-figured queen, and his already engorged cock swelled to near painful proportions. Even his wildest fantasies hadn't prepared him for the reality of having her all to himself without the complications of their family's animosity. She was his, at least for two weeks, and despite how it came about, despite his earlier reservations he planned to make the most of every minute.

Being at the site today and knowing she was in his home had nearly undone him. He'd made some minor errors that could have easily snowballed if not for the very competent staff of people working with him. He wouldn't make the same mistake, tomorrow because he planned on keeping a very naked Lynn in bed until he could work her out of his system. From his body's reaction, there would definitely be some mandatory overtime on order.

"Take off your robe," he instructed gently as she stood at the hot tub's edge looking like the African goddess of all things sensual. If there wasn't such a deity he'd certainly nominate her for the position.

He saw her hesitation and was prepared to insist when she pulled the knot at the front of the robe loose in one fluid motion. The material fluttered to the hard concrete in a gentle cascade and Jake thought he would come apart right there amidst the gurgling water. She was phenomenal. He'd prided himself over the years on liking women in all shapes and sizes, but none could come close to her. Plump, round breasts stood proudly, nipples already pebbled. His gaze fixated on the dark twins as her chest rose and fell in a deep even pattern. Her waist dipped but gave way to wide hips that were meant to be held while he rode her. A tiny thatch of trimmed hair in the shape of a miniscule triangle seemed to serve as a directional beacon. If ever there was a woman meant for some serious loving, she was it.

"Come here."

She moved forward, stopping at the water's edge to dip one foot in.

"No, come to me," he said slowly.

She did as instructed, walking around the circular tub to stand inches from him.

"Turn around so I can see that beautiful ass."

He was pleased with how easily she followed instructions. Yes, he'd found a rare treasure indeed.

"You see the towels?" He indicated the thick, fluffed and folded cloths on either side of his shoulders.

"Yes."

"That's were I want you to place your knees."

Lynn looked at him over her shoulder in surprise.

"Do as you're told, Lynn, this is the last warning I'll give you."

With what he knew was great care she straddled his face, resting her knees on the towels he provided as a cushion for her comfort.

Her nether regions hovered just inches above his face and he inhaled her musky woman's scent as if it were the finest of perfumes.

"You may hold on to the rail for leverage," he offered, wetting his lips in anticipation.

* * * *

This isn't happening, Lynn thought, grabbing onto the thick metal railing. She couldn't possibly be on her knees with Jake's face positioned below her crotch. The bubbles and steam from the hot tub warmed her feet and ankles.

"Lower yourself."

She did, feeling fingers spread her folds wide for his invasion.

A rush of desire hit her with such force, at the first swipe of his tongue on her clit she was certain her legs would buckle. His next strokes came in rapid successions, tickling her nub until she moaned out loud. Heaven help her, but she loved the swirling of his firm tongue on her distended flesh. As if possessing a mind of their own, her hips pumped over him, grinding the swollen flesh against his exquisite lapping.

"Yes Jake...yes," she moaned.

When he slid a finger into her now steaming core she thought she was a goner for certain. The peak was near she could feel it just as sure as the titillating tongue that was driving her to it.

"No," she cried when his delicious teasing abruptly ceased.

"In the water." The order came out roughly against her juice soaked folds.

With great care, and assistance from Jake's powerful arms, she slipped down his body and into the water. No sooner was she in the hot depths his arms encircled her waist and his mouth claimed hers for a near brutal kiss. She didn't mind one iota as she pulled him closer with arms locked around his neck. His cock nestled between them like a thick rod, and Lynn made sure to grind against him with her stomach.

"I gotta have you." He was already repositioning her as he ground out the words. She allowed herself to be easily manipulated into a position that would have her back pressed against the hardness of his chest.

"Open for me."

She did, spreading her legs as wide as possible to allow him full access to her hungry core. She didn't have long to wait before Jake impaled her with his thick, stiff cock, filling and stretching her beyond belief.

"Oohh!" The scream manifested itself before she could catch it.

Jake held her in place with firm hands guiding her hips over him as if he thought to fit more of his cock in her.

He stilled, nipping her neck while he pulsated inside her tight core.

"Are you ready for more, sweetling?"

She couldn't speak, but managed a nod.

"Good." He pushed more of himself into her welcoming sheath until she was completely seated on his lap.

"All mine," he groaned. His roughened hands instructed her hips until she picked up on his rhythm. He surged into her several times before gaining momentum. "Only mine."

She jerked when he latched on to her neck, suckling the flesh until it throbbed.

Lynn was frantic now. As if his plundering cock and sucking mouth weren't enough, he dropped the arm around her waist, allowing his fingers to dip between her folds until he found her nub.

"Do you want to come?" he rasped in her ear. Her neck still tingled where he'd released her flesh seconds earlier.

"Yes, please," she met his lunges with fervor.

"God, I don't ever want to stop fucking you." The words sounded strained, letting her know he was just as close to his own climax as she was to hers.

"I'm coming," she yelled into the night air when her orgasm slammed into her. Her muscles clenched rapidly around his still plundering cock, but it wasn't long before Jake was howling his own completion.

"Aahh!" He shot into her in a series of spasms, his cock jumping deep in the confines of her heat, his thick seed coating her womb over and over until there was nothing left.

Lynn didn't protest when he pulled her limp body across his lap. Her breaths came in quick shallow repetition as her pulse gradually came under control.

He planted several kisses from her forehead to light caresses on her lips.

She felt as if she could have fallen asleep right there in his arms, surrounded by the soothing swirling effects of the heated water. It was another perfect Texas night. The sky above was dark and speckled by ever emerging stars. She was certain that nothing could beat the rightness of the moment. For years she thought that the reality of making love with Jake wouldn't compare to her wildest fantasies. Boy, had she been wrong on that count.

"Jake!" she screeched as he lifted them from the steaming pool. "What are you doing?"

"Taking you to bed, where I can indulge in that delectable body of yours some more."

"I can walk." She didn't try to conceal her excitement at what he suggested.

"You could."

Lynn was in awe with how simply he carried her through the house and up the stairs to his bedroom, without showing the slightest sign of tiring. She giggled when he purposefully bounced her on the center of the bed. She doubted any of her past lovers could have carried her more than a few feet even if they wanted to, but this was Jake Rangell.

She sobered slowly as he stood at the foot of the bed, watching her with a quiet concentration that had her feeling suddenly shy. Reaching for a pillow to shield herself, she wondered if he was regretting their wild coupling.

"Don't," he snapped, halting her as she zeroed in on her plump target. "Never hide yourself from me, is that understood?"

She could only nod her response, trying to will away her unease at laying there nude. Little comfort was taken in the fact that he stood in all his naked glory as well, because quite frankly the man was pure perfection. His brawny chest was flawlessly sculptured, tapering down to contoured abs. She'd never cared much for hair on a man, but the dark fur on him only added to his sex appeal. She caught her breath at the first true glimpse of his manhood, on the verge of reawakening. It was the largest thing she'd seen on any man. It was no wonder she'd felt stretched beyond belief with him inside her. She wasn't sure if she'd let him near her earlier if she'd seen what was in store.

"Bend your knees and open up those lovely legs for me."

Her eyes shot up to his again at the directive. He was serious. Obedience had never been a strong suit of hers, not with just any man, but then again he wasn't just any man. Knees dropped until they each laid on their respective piece of bedding, and she closed her eyes at the brazen picture she was sure she projected.

"Look at me, Lynn." His voice was gentle, but there was an edge to it, as if he were fighting for patience.

Her eyes rounded at the sight of him standing there, stroking his swollen cock while his eyes devoured her.

"I want you to touch yourself, remember how it felt to ride my tongue."

He had to be kidding. Her eyes darted down to the beast between his fingers. The damned thing looked as if it were still growing.

"I can't, not with you watching me," she squeaked. Obviously he didn't have the same problem.

"You will because it's what I want you to do. Now put your hand between your legs, Lynn."

Lord, what is wrong with me, she thought as she edged fingers between her splayed thighs, all the while holding his gaze.

"That's it, now use your index finger and find the thick little clit of yours."

She did with the ease of several years practice on her side.

"Good, now stroke it for me."

She made several tentative rubs, watching as his excitement seemed to parallel with her manipulations.

"Harder," he ordered.

"Ahh," she gasped at the rising pleasure that was rapidly replacing embarrassment.

"That's it, sweetling, I can see how wet you're getting. Touch that hot little pussy so you can feel those juices on your fingers."

She was wet, so damn wet and horny as hell. She rubbed her clit again now in tandem with his stroking, dipping two fingers in her warmth as instructed.

"Oohh, yes."

"You can't cum yet, sweetling."

He had to be fucking kidding. Another wave of pleasure shot through her.

"Lock your hands above your head."

What?

"Do it now or I will have to punish you."

Punish? What was he talking about?

"Lynn." His voice was firmer this time, and she realized that he'd stopped stroking his now massive penis that jutted in front of him.

She ceased her own ministrations with a frustrated cry. What the hell kind of game was he playing at, getting her all hot and bothered — never mind that it was at her own hand — then just letting her down.

"Sadistic bastard," she muttered, ready to roll over and secure herself in his bathroom. At least there she could finish in peace.

"Not quite, but if that's what you want…"

Before she could respond he was on the bed, wedged between her thick thighs.

"Let me go." She jerked as her hands were captured and secured above her head in one of his strong ones.

"I believe it's time I started your instruction, sweetling."

"What are you talking about?" She made another unsuccessful attempt at jerking her trapped hands free, upset with herself for feeling turned on.

"Before we started this I let you know I expected you to do whatever I requested and I meant it. Now, let's discuss the consequences of your not following my instructions."

Lynn's mind was reeling over his words. Consequences?

"For deliberate disobedience you will get five lashes."

"Lashes? I don't know what kind of kinky sex stuff you're into, Jake Rangell, but if for one moment you think I'm going to let you hit me you have another think coming."

She'd learned a lot since leaving her family's ranch, had met men and women who were into the Dominant/submissive lifestyle. She'd even done some mild experimentation with it herself, but found she couldn't truly have a relationship with a man who wanted her to humiliate him in the bedroom. Not to mention being dominated by men who were nothing but veritable mooches, wanting a woman to provide for them in exchange for some "out there" sexual encounters.

"And what do you think you can do to stop me sweetling? Struggle, scream perhaps? I think we both know that would be futile."

"I wondered why you were still alone after all these years. I guess now I have my answer."

"That sassy mouth of yours will earn you extra lashes."

"Try it and—" With speed and coordination that didn't seem humanly possible, Lynn found herself face down on the bed, arms secured behind her at the wrist by one of Jake's hands. A muscled leg was thrown across her own to minimize her movements.

"You were saying?"

"That you're a big fat jerk and I don't care if...ooohhh."

She tensed as Jake's free hand squeezed between her thighs, pressing forward until he found his intended target between her woman's folds.

"Stop," she croaked, hating herself for the instant heat that rushed to her clit.

"Is that what you really want?" He rubbed one finger back and forth over the distended nub, adding to her already aroused state.

"Yesss," she hissed. Her hips pressed into his tormenting finger.

He stroked her one last time before pulling his hand from beneath her now quivering body.

"I hate you," she spat in frustration.

"It doesn't have to be this way, sweetling. I can give you the pleasure we both want so badly." He released her wrists.

"But at what price?" she mumbled into the bed as the weight of his leg was removed.

"The price is that you give yourself to me completely," he said easily. Lynn shuddered with desire as one hand began to massage her round ass in firm fistfuls.

"And the spanking stuff?"

"That's up to you. I am not an unfair man, but know this: I punish just as easily as I reward."

Lynn laid there in quiet contemplation, without saying the words she knew what he was asking. The question was could she do it, even for two weeks?

"I don't know if I can be a submissive," she thought aloud.

"With the right man you'll do just fine."

"And you think you're the right one for me."

"I'm the only one for you."

Lynn turned over on her side. "Just for the two weeks, and then we go back to normal."

"We'll see." The look on his face was indefinable.

"Okay," she finally agreed, turning on her back to resume the position he'd requested of her earlier. "I'm yours."

His gaze raked her body slowly. "All mine."

He took his position between her legs. "I believe I've been very remiss in my care of you."

"Oh."

Fingers crept up her abdomen, past her rib cage to the full globes of her breasts. He tweaked each nipple with his fingers, causing her to shiver in response.

"Time for me to rectify that oversight."

And rectify is exactly what he did. He leaned over her to take one hard nipple between his lips, stroking it with his tongue until she begged him for more. Pressing the plump flesh of her breast together gave him access to both pebbled peaks at once and he took full advantage sucking until she writhed beneath him.

"Please, Jake, I can't take anymore."

"It's okay, sweetling," he consoled, positioning himself over her hot, dripping core. He gave her one long, deep kiss before sinking completely into her welcoming body with one fluid thrust.

"So tight," he groaned. "You were made for me."

He retreated and pushed further into her.

"You're so big," she crooned, thrusting her hips forward for his next lunge.

"That's it, give it to me."

She matched him thrust for excruciatingly exquisite thrust. Lynn thought she would implode from the repeat pleasure of him sinking into her body.

"Oh, yes," she cried. Her vaginal walls suctioned around him, inviting him to fill her completely.

"All mine!" he yelled as the orgasm took hold of him. He shot his load deep within the confines of her body, hammering away until he was completely spent.

Four

Lynn woke up alone. A glance at the bedside clock let her know it was after eight in the morning, well past the beginning of a workday for ranchers. She laid in the warm confines of the bed, debating whether to get up now or sleep a little longer. Jake had kept her up for the better part of the night with his demanding sex drive, and she had eagerly and wantonly complied. A few more minutes and she would get up, she told herself.

Dammit, she'd forgotten to talk with Jake about something to do while she was there. She didn't think she could handle another day of nothingness.

Seconds ticked into minutes and Lynn knew she couldn't lie in bed any longer. Maybe Jake hadn't gotten that much of a head start on her and she could catch up with him. There was bound to be plenty of things she could do to help out, but first she would grab a quick shower and something to eat. A night of physical activity definitely left a girl famished.

* * * *

Lynn screeched at the top of her lungs as the glass shower door jerked open and Jake stepped in with her.

"I swear I'm buying you a bell," she cried, letting the warm spray wash the soap out of her eyes.

She'd been in the process of washing her hair, eyes closed, when he came into the bathroom, and didn't see him as he slipped quietly into the open shower.

"What are you doing here anyway?" she sputtered, wiping remnants of water from her eyes.

"It's my house," he replied, giving her one of his sexy Jake smiles.

"I thought you were out working."

"You sound disappointed."

"Not at all." She wrapped arms around his waist. "Actually, I'm glad you're still here. It saves me traipsing all over this damned ranch to find you."

"Find me for what?" He kissed her forehead.

"I need a project or something while I'm here. I was bored out of my mind yesterday."

"I think I have a few ideas on how to keep you busy." He poked her with his already protruding cock which she'd tried to ignore, at least until she had the matter of daytime activity out of the way.

"I'm serious, Jake."

"So am I, sweetling," he replied, backing her up against a sleek tiled wall.

* * * *

He dried her off and took her back into the bedroom, where a smorgasbord of food on a tray lay on the bed for them.

"You did this?"

"Of course, I have to see to all the needs of my woman."

His woman. Her stomach fluttered at the very idea.

They ate, teased, and eventually ended up putting the tray on the floor so Jake could show her just how enjoyable being a human serving tray was.

Hours later, Lynn woke up for a second time that day alone, only this time the clock let her know that it was just after noon. She bound from bed, admonishing herself for sleeping so late.

Lynn straightened the bed, surprised to see the remains of their earlier meal cleaned away. Once the bed passed her inspection she opted for another quick shower. This time Jake didn't join her and as much as she didn't want to admit it, his absence left her feeling lonely.

She dressed in her standard pair of jeans and a button-up blouse, she took the time to blow dry her short hair before pushing a head band over the thick strands to keep them in place.

She ran into Helen as she left the bedroom.

"You didn't happen to see Jake before he left?"

"He didn't leave, he's in his study."

"Really?" Lynn couldn't believe her good fortune, for the second time that day she was saved from taking one his trucks and driving around the ranch to look for him.

"Am I interrupting anything?" she asked, peeking around the office door after a brief knock.

Jake looked up from the stack of papers he was poring over.

"Not anything that I don't want to be taken from, come in."

Lynn noted he wore a regular white T-shirt today, and although she couldn't tell from his position, was certain jeans covered his bottom half.

"Stay there, please," she stopped him as he rose. "I know if you touch me I won't ever get out what I've been trying to ask."

He quirked a brow in her direction but didn't comment on her request other than to say, "Okay, shoot."

"I was hoping that I could help out with something on your ranch. I'm not savvy with the oil end of the business, but I'm a quick learner and would love the practice. I'm sure I can help Logan when I get back."

"No."

"No?"

"It's what I said." The expression on his face was unrelenting.

"Why not, or are you afraid of having the competition traipsing around your land?"

"Not at all, feel free to pick my brain over anything you want about the oil business."

"Well, why can't I help out? I grew up on a ranch, for God's sake. I'm not afraid of a little hard work."

"I won't have you 'traipsing,' as you call it, around the men. A lot of them don't go to town for several weeks on end, and I don't need you there to distract them," he answered. "I'd hate to have to break someone's nose and lose a good employee at the same time."

"Well, that's just ridiculous. I've worked along side the men at The Harrington all my life without incident."

He shrugged. "I'm sorry, I'm not going to risk it."

"Okay, then I'll go help out Logan. I can coordinate with him so Daddy doesn't know I haven't left town."

"No."

She crossed arms stubbornly over her chest.

"And why not?"

"Because you belong here, with me."

"I will be here with you, after work," she explained.

"I've already given you my answer."

"So you expect me to twiddle my thumbs every day for the next two weeks until you come home."

"No, I plan on spending as much time here as possible. As you can see, I have plenty of paperwork to keep me busy."

"So what do I do?"

Jake sighed. "If you feel that you have to have something to do, you can help me with getting this quarter's financials squared away for my auditors."

"You mean it?" She was taken aback at the suggestion. Why would he trust her with something as important as that?

"That's if you feel up to it."

"You're kidding, right, when do I start?"

* * * *

Jake looked up from the spreadsheets Lynn just printed out, watching as her fingers flew over the keypad to enter another series of numbers and formulas on the database. They'd been working for two hours straight without a break. She hadn't even so much as spared him a sideways glance and he didn't like it, not one bit. As absurd as it was he actually thought he was jealous of his financial statements. He could barely stay focused on the figures, wanting instead to push all the papers off the desk and take her right there. He couldn't get enough. Like a new addict after the first taste, he was hooked.

Heaven help him, but he would be content locked away in his home with her for the next two weeks, exploring every possibility. He didn't want to share her with his reports, let alone other people. Jake never considered himself a jealous person, not by a long shot, but the thought of her working side by side with his men was unsettling. And as for her lovesick stepbrother, well, he didn't want to leave anything to chance on that front.

"It's quitting time, Lynn."

"Just a couple more minutes, I'm almost done," she answered without looking up from her task.

"Sweetling, we can begin again tomorrow. At the rate you're going you'll be done in a week."

"Okay, just one more thing." Her fingers continued their rapid pounding.

Jake sighed, knowing the only way she would stop is if he took matters into his own hands.

"Hey, what are you doing?" She swiped at him as he used the mouse to hit the save icon and exit the system.

"We're done working for the day. I thought we'd go to town and catch a movie."

"A movie. I haven't been to the movies since I've been back."

Jake bit back his response. He doubted she'd done much for herself since she'd come home. Another twinge of jealousy hit him at how much she sacrificed for the Harringtons. He wondered if they even appreciated all her efforts.

"What do you have in mind?"

"Your choice, but we'd better get going or we'll end up having to catch some late showing," he urged.

"Let me just grab my purse and I'll be ready." She bound out the room, and he couldn't stop himself from watching her go.

The movie suggestion had been a last minute idea that popped into his head. He'd have much preferred to take her upstairs and make love to her like the night before, but he felt the need to show her more than sex. When they parted in a couple weeks he wanted it to be just as hard of her as he knew it would be for him.

* * * *

They compromised on a romantic comedy starring one of her favorite actresses, although Lynn found herself having a hard time focusing with Jake absently rubbing the back of her hand. It was an innocent gesture, should have probably been soothing, but it left her wanting him to touch more of her, to feel his strong hands all over her body.

"Are you okay?" Jake asked as they left the theatre.

"Yes, why do you ask?" They walked leisurely to his SUV, holding hands.

"Well, I've asked you twice how you liked the movie and so far nothing."

"I'm sorry." She was genuinely apologetic. "Just lost in thought."

"Share with me."

"Nothing really, just a bunch of random thoughts," she supplied after a momentary hesitation. She didn't want to admit to him that her thoughts were centered on all the things they would do to each other later.

"Hmm, maybe I can help bring them back in the moment." He stopped short on the walking path and pulled her into his arms. One finger tilted her chin up before he dipped his head to her own. Their lips brushed in a gentle kiss, before Jake stepped things up a notch urging her mouth open with his own. It ended all too soon.

"What are you thinking about now?" he asked. Neither paid attention to the passersby.

"More of that."

"Good. Now let's go eat."

"You have a ton of food in that fridge of yours," she reminded.

"You're right, I do, but I think that will be the last thing on either of our minds as soon as that front door closes."

He was right, of course, because as things stood now she was ready to jump his bones and didn't care who was around.

Garrett County had experienced some rapid growth since she'd last been home, so much so that Lynn felt like an outsider now. When Jake suggested that they get something to eat her mind swam with the numerous suggestions he rattled off. In the end they opted on a trendy burger joint that Jake swore made the best burgers and milkshakes in three counties.

"So, was I right?"

"I'm not sure if I should admit that to you. I mean, I do have to think about the ramifications of such a statement."

He nodded in mock sincerity. "Would set the women's movement back a few years, ya think?"

"More like a millennia. We do have a credo, several in fact."

"The first of which being 'never tell a man he's right'?"

"That's the second one actually." She smiled at him, enjoying their conversation. Around them the restaurant hummed. Teens chatted a little loudly at one booth, young couples with children sat at others, a few elderly patrons gathered in groups while another treated a grandchild to an evening shake.

"The first is never let him find out he's right, the second is never tell him he is. A little redundant, but I think it gets the point across."

"Hmm, well, how about I just base my answer on the way you're wolfing down the burger."

"Hey, ladies don't wolf their food," she said before taking another drink of her milkshake.

His only answer was to chuckle before taking a generous bite from his own burger.

"I've been curious about something, Jake."

"What's that?"

"Well, why aren't you married, for starters. I would have thought by now you'd have a wife and a couple of kids under your belt."

He crooked his head. "Just never met the right woman, I guess."

"And who would the right woman be for Jake Rangell?"

"Good question. Someone who's intelligent, warm, caring, an eager lover. Who isn't afraid to give fully of herself to her mate."

He stared directly at her as he spoke the words, and Lynn tried swallowing the lump that formed in her throat.

"Well, I'm sure half the women in Garrett County could fit that description."

"No, the woman that I'm looking for is a true diamond in the rough. What about you? I was equally surprised to learn that you hadn't married yet."

"Just never came up, I guess."

"An interesting choice of words."

"Well, I was seeing someone in Arizona. Nothing really serious, just casual dating," she revealed.

"How casual?"

Lynn felt suddenly uncomfortable under his unwavering gaze.

She shrugged. "We saw each other off and on for about a year, shared some of the same interests and it just became very comfortable getting together."

"Sounds boring."

"To some, I guess. Leo is a man who lives by practical principles."

"And is that what you're looking for in a man, Lynn, practicality?"

"Maybe to a certain degree I am, but I want someone with a sense of loyalty over order. With passion, honor, and an inner strength that manifests itself in everything he's about."

"And Leo didn't possess that?"

She chuckled. "Hardly, but I guess what killed it was his inability to understand my need to return home to help my family. According to him my obligations and ties to the Harringtons died with my mother."

Jake shook his head. "I wouldn't go that far, but I don't like the position they've put you in."

"If you're having second thoughts about our arrangement, you could drop me off at The Harrington tonight. We'll find another way to—"

The rest of her thought died in her throat as Jake suddenly stood, taking several bills out of his fold and dropping them on the table.

"Let's go," he said, pulling her chair back. Lynn's heart caught in her throat at his abrupt actions. That was it? He was done with her and ready to eagerly drop her off with her family. No sooner were they back in the warm early evening air Jake grabbed her hand and stalked off through the open plaza, leaving Lynn no choice but to keep up with his long-legged pace.

"Jake?" she questioned as he lead her into the alcove of a building.

"My truck is too damned far away, and I wanted some privacy for what I want to say and do."

"You mean you're not taking me back The Harrington?"

"Not by a long shot. I plan on seeing this thing out until the very end," he answered, his mouth inches from her own. She could feel his fingers pulling buttons free on her blouse.

"Jake, we can't." Her pulse raced with the excitement of moment. "Someone could come by."

"So let them," he rasped before taking her lips in a hard kiss. He pushed her further into the shadows of the building, blocking her view of the plaza, and effectively shielding her from passersby.

She was drowning, sinking into the abyss of Jake. He'd only undone a few buttons on the bottom of her shirt to allow him access to the bare flesh of her stomach. His work roughened hands traveled up and down her torso before dropping to the clasp of her jeans. Jake's kiss became more demanding as he plundered her mouth, taking everything thing that she offered, yet demanding even more. Lynn groaned as fingers dipped between the elastic of her panties. There was no pretense in his actions as Jake zeroed in on her thick clit, massaging, stroking until she became a quaking mass.

"That's it, ride it, baby." He pulled back long enough to utter the brief sentence before reclaiming her mouth, his tongue mimicking the movements of his fingers.

She was ready to die from the wonderful sensations, as he stroked her clit in firm circular motions. Her orgasm hit her fast and hard. Jake muffled her cry of completion with his mouth while he fondled her until her body succumbed to its last bout of shudders.

"Omigod," Lynn said between ragged breaths, slumping against the wall for support. "We shouldn't have done that here," she uttered more to herself while he refastened her jeans.

A finger under her chin had her staring up into his smoldering gaze. "Don't ever regret anything we do together, sweetling. Not when it feels that good. Do you understand?"

"Yes."

"Good." He bent to retrieve her purse the she hadn't known she'd dropped. "Now, let's go home."

* * * *

"Thank you for tonight," Lynn said as they prepared for bed that evening. Her mind still reeled from their near public display. She doubted that she should be enjoying Jake's company so much under the circumstances, but couldn't help herself.

"You don't need to thank me." He encircled her from behind, taking the nightgown out of her hands and tossing it to the floor. "And you won't be needing this." His stiff manhood pressed into her lower back through denim.

He brushed kisses against the nape of her neck in slow patterns while unbuttoning her blouse.

"I thought I would jump in the shower first."

"Not necessary."

He shushed her protest.

"Tonight I want you to ride me," he whispered, pulling the blouse away from her chocolaty flesh. "And I want to watch these lovelies bounce." He unsnapped her bra, effortlessly allowing her breasts to spill out before promptly cupping them in large hands.

Lynn sighed as she leaned into him. Her lids drooped heavily.

God, she loved this man's touch. He was definitely going to be a hard habit to break.

The shrill sound of the phone filled the room eliciting a groan from both of them.

"I'll let it ring."

Lynn wanted to agree but thought better of it. "It's late, it could be important."

"More important than this?" He gave her breasts a firm squeeze.

"It could be about Race."

"All right," he agreed, disengaging himself reluctantly.

"Jake," he bit, waiting for the caller to get to the point. "This had better be important, Harrington."

Lynn perked up, holding out her hand expectantly.

"She's right here, can this wait until tomorrow? We are on our way to bed."

Lynn's reproachful look spoke volumes but Jake looked unfazed.

"Fine, make it quick."

She practically snatched the phone when he finally offered the cordless to her.

"Is everything okay?"

"Yeah," came Logan's reply. "Who the hell does that guy think he is, screening your calls?"

With Jake staring at her, she ignored the question, "Is Daddy okay?"

"Yeah he's fine. He can't wait for you to come home, and neither can I"

"It won't be long."

She kept her eyes on Jake, who'd begun the task of undressing but making it obvious that he was listening to every word.

"What did you call for?" She didn't want to rush Logan, but knew Jake's patience wouldn't last long especially since he harbored some warped notion that her stepbrother had romantic feelings for her, if that didn't beat all.

"I stopped by tonight to get you. I think I've found a way for us to get the equipment we need from another source."

"What?"

"You weren't there, where were you?" he questioned.

"A movie and dinner. What other source?"

"Tony Kilpatrick."

"The loan shark?" she stopped herself from shrieking.

"That's just a rumor," he defended.

"One that can be substantiated by people with injuries."

"Well, it's better than you selling your body. Unless, of course, you like being with Rangell under these circumstances?"

The man in question stood several feet from her of her, nude and looking none too pleased by the direction her side of the conversation was heading in.

"Well?" Logan asked expectantly.

"No, of course not," she lied.

"So, I'll swing by now and get you. We can call Tony in the morning."

"No," she rushed. "Logan, I'll call you tomorrow first thing. Promise me you won't do anything silly."

"I'll wait to hear from you," he agreed.

She let out a long breath. "Okay, goodnight, Logan."

"Night, Twittle."

She ended the connection feeling uneasy about their conversation.

"That didn't sound anything like the cockamamie excuse he gave me, so what was that about?"

"Ranch stuff. I'll talk with him in the morning," she dismissed.

"I hope he isn't thinking to get you involved in anything else. I won't allow it," Jake said with all seriousness.

"It's nothing I can't handle."

"That's what I'm afraid of Lynn. Invite Logan out here tomorrow. I want to hear what he has to say myself."

She knew there was no way her brother would go for that.

"I'll see what I can do."

"I mean it, Lynn, I don't want you getting involved in anymore of your brothers' screw ups. Let me deal with Logan."

He had to know what he was asking was impossible.

"Enough about him. I need to be inside of you soon or I won't be responsible for my actions." He advanced on her swiftly, crossing the short distance.

"Jake," she giggled as he easily hoisted her over his shoulder eating up a path to his bed.

Five

Lynn was awakened by the feel of Jake's large thigh wedged between her own. The heat from his body warmed her back in the air-conditioned room. She'd actually thought she was having another very erotic dream, staring her new lover. When her fuzzy brain finally registered that there was more reality involved in invoking those blissful sensations, he was already gliding inside her wet core.

"Hmm," she purred. Jake teased her nipples, only heightening her pleasure.

"You feel so good." He leveraged himself on one elbow, positioning himself for deeper penetration.

"I can't get enough of you," he murmured into her ear while administering lingering plunges. "God help me." He drug out their orgasms until they were both a clammy mass of tremors.

* * * *

Sitting at Jake's desk, she shook off the memories of their early morning play. She was alone now — Jake had gone to check on things at his sites, leaving her to his financial statements. He promised to return at lunchtime and she looked forward to his homecoming. Lynn looked at the clock on the computer, that was a good four hours away, enough time to talk with Logan and make a considerable dent in the paperwork in front of her.

She tried her brother's cell phone first, knowing at this late morning hour he'd be hard at work. He answered on the third ring.

"Hello," he snapped.

"Logan, it's me."

"Oh, sorry, Twittle. I saw the caller ID and thought it was that damned Rangell again, he left a message earlier."

"What did he say?" Jake hadn't mentioned anything.

"Nothing worth repeating, but I do want you away from him as soon as possible."

Lynn was curious as to what Jake called her brother about, but didn't want to hear Logan rag on him. She chose to ignore his irritation. "How are things going?"

He paused. "Slowly, at the moment. One of the men walked out this morning, which is going to set us back considerably."

"What about Ryan?"

"Are you kidding me?" He huffed. "I sent him back to work on the fences. I'm going to have to put an ad in the paper for three more men if we're to stay on target."

"Three?"

"One part- and two full-timers. We were already in need, and now with Jasper gone we'll be in a serious hurt."

"Logan, I'm not sure that we can afford that. Replacing him, okay, but another person will be stretching it, and I don't want to hear any more talk about going to Tony Kilpatrick."

"I didn't mean that. I had a little too much to drink last night."

"Well, I hope you slept it off, because a loan shark is not the option. Listen, until we figure this out why don't I come help out?"

Logan chuckled on the other end. "Twittle, this is no work for a woman."

"Logan Ambrose Harrington, I'm going to pretend I didn't hear that. I'm coming right over."

Lynn found the keys to Jake's two other pickups and SUV in the garage hanging in plain sight. For a brief moment she contemplated calling him, but thought better of it. Knowing him, he'd just try to talk her out of going to The Harrington, but this was a family matter and that came first to her.

* * * *

Logan shook his head at the approaching woman. "What do you think you're doing?"

"I told you, I'm here to help, what else?"

"And Rangell let you come?"

"Let's get some things straight. First off, Jake doesn't *let* me do anything, I'm my own woman. Our arrangement is a business one."

"So, you didn't tell him." He smiled down at her, blue eyes laughing.

"Shut up. Is Daddy up at the house?"

"Yeah, I promised to bring him out later in the week. I wanted to wait until we were well into production, but at this rate..." he trailed off. What he didn't say spoke volumes. Time was of the essence.

"Well what are we standing around for, there's work to be done."

"All right."

* * * *

He was going to wring her sexy little neck, right after he killed Logan Harrington, because he was certain the man was the reason behind her disappearance. Jake raged silently, retracing his steps back to his work truck.

All morning thoughts of her consumed him, and not just the kind that had his cock stirring, although those visited him many times, too. Truth be told, he just wanted to be around her, to catch the way her eye followed him, to see the smile on her face and ecstasy in her eyes. He couldn't wait to get home that afternoon, had driven at record speed only to be greeted by an empty house. A note on his office computer confirmed the suspicion that had already taken root in his mind. She'd gone back to the Harrington because of Jake.

> *Something's come up at home, I'll be back later.*
> *Lynn*

He'd promptly balled the piece of paper up in agitation, unhappy with Lynn's waywardness. He doubted anything happened to Race—she would have called him for that. No, this vanishing act had Logan written all over it. Jake cursed under his breath as he thought back to the conversation of the night before. If the pinhead involved her in some dangerous, hair-brained venture he would rip him apart, had already told him as much in his morning call.

* * * *

"Feed it some more line," one of the crew hands called, and Lynn activated the button that would send more cable down the ominous looking hole in the ground.

"Okay, that's enough," he yelled over the loud machinery.

She hit the switch again effectively, bringing the beast to a halt.

"Looking good," the foreman said. "Why don't we break for lunch?"

There would be no objections from her. Up until that moment she'd hauled and dug right along side the men while her brother stomped around, shaking his head at her. It was the foreman who'd finally suggested she come and help out with the equipment. She knew from watching that it was a one man task, but it was their way of giving her a break without offending.

"Well, that fella looks angrier than a wet hen," an unidentified man called, causing everyone in hearing range to look up from their task of securing the site before breaking.

"Fuck," Logan mumbled. He stood next to her, stretching to his full six foot height. Until that point Lynn hadn't paid much attention, but now she looked to where everyone was gawking.

She cursed under her breath at the fuming face of Jake Rangell as he made his way towards them. Dust settled around his truck where he swung in seconds earlier, boxing in other pickups.

"I'll handle this, Twittle," Logan said before making his way to intercept the cross man whose eyes had zeroed in on their target.

"Hell, little lady, what did you do to get Jake's panties in a bunch?" Kirk, a long time ranch hand, said for her ears only.

Lynn was rendered silent by Jakes unwavering stare. *This doesn't bode well*, she thought, her mind racing for a plausible explanation that she hoped would appease him. With Jake nearly fifteen yards away, she knew she'd better think fast.

"Logan is either crazy or very brave," Kirk continued.

Lynn's eyes rounded as she and the others witnessed a train wreck in the making.

"Logan," she called, hurrying behind him. "Wait, let me talk to him."

"Stay out of this, Lynn." He didn't spare her a backwards glance. Jake, on the other hand, couldn't seem to tear his gaze away from her.

"Logan!" She jerked on his arm, effectively stopping him in his tracks. "I don't want to exaggerate this anymore than it already is," she said.

"Go get in the truck, Lynn." Jake's voice was surprisingly calm, and she peeked around Logan's broad shoulders to make sure she hadn't assessed the situation incorrectly just moments before.

Nope, he was pissed.

"Hi, Jake," she said, stepping around her brother, pushing him arms distance behind her. "I was just—"

"You were disobeying me again, now get in the truck." He stopped, leaving enough space between them for her not to have to crane her neck to look at his irritated visage.

She bit back her immediate response, remembering the goal was to deescalate things.

"Now just wait a minute, you can't order my sister around like she's your property."

"No?" For the first time Jake acknowledged the younger man, fixing him with his steely brown eyed gaze.

"Hey, if you're upset about the truck I'll just take it back to Rangell Ranch. I'm sorry, I know I should have asked permission before taking it."

His attention shifted back to her. "You know I didn't come for the truck."

A sinking feeling in her stomach had her retreating back.

"Just say the word, Lynn," Logan said from behind her.

"I'd love nothing more, Harrington." Jake accepted the man's tacit challenge.

"Hell, this is better than pay-per-view," came a comment from one of the men, who now gathered at a safe distance from the potential brawl.

Bravery she didn't quite feel had her speaking up. "I'll go with him."

"No, Lynn, let's just end this all here and now."

"We can't." She didn't bother to turn around.

"In the truck, Lynn. I'll send someone for the other one later."

"Jake, perhaps I could just stay a little longer to help out with—"

"Don't make this any worse than it already is."

With all eyes on her, she marched to the dusty pickup Jake arrived in, leaving Logan to gnash his teeth and the crew of The Harrington to wonder what the hell had just happened.

During the silent drive back to Rangell Ranch, Lynn experienced a plethora of emotions ranging from anger and dread to fear. It was the last emotion that gripped her as they pulled up to Jake's home. Although she doubted he would do anything to cause her injury, she was fairly certain her little transgression would warrant some form of punishment in his eye. He ushered her from the oversized truck and into the entrance of the house.

"Logan needed my help," she started as soon as the door closed behind them.

"Go upstairs and wash that dirt off you, then wait for me on the bed."

She could have protested, but was so grateful to get a few moments alone she almost took the steps two at a time.

Anger was the next of the emotions to surface as she dried off from her shower.

What right did he have to be upset with her, she'd done nothing wrong! It was obvious he didn't care that she took his old, beat up jalopy, so what real reason did he have to be angry? Okay, he wanted her to play the submissive role in the bedroom, but he couldn't honestly think that would extend to everyday life.

She found her night shirt hanging up in the closet again and pulled it over her head. If he thought she was going to be waiting naked in his bed he had another think coming, she huffed to herself.

Instead she settled into an oversized chair near the picture window, overlooking the enormous range.

Some twenty minutes later Jake entered the bedroom carrying a tray loaded with fruits, breads, and other food she couldn't make out at her angle. His gaze stopped immediately on the empty bed, then scanned the room until it landed on her. She saw the tension in his jaw as he went to place the tray on the bedside table, before making his way before heading in her direction, back to the door.

"I think we should talk about today..." Her words trailed off when she found herself scooped up and tossed over his shoulder like a sack of potatoes. Her night shirt rode up over hips, exposing her bare ass.

"Put me down!" she screeched.

His answer was to deliver a stinging blow to her bare bottom.

She yelped in surprise that he'd actually administered the strike, but even more at how painful the contact was. The after effects of it left her flesh throbbing.

"You bastard!"

Whack!

Her eyes misted over with tears this time, but she willed them not to fall.

Another crack was delivered, followed by two more.

"That was for not following my most recent instructions," he said, rubbing her bruised rear before setting her on the bed. "Sit up."

She did quietly, sitting back on her haunches, hating the lone tear that rolled down her face.

"Get rid of the shirt."

She hesitated briefly before pulling the top over her head. Jake took the silky material from her, using the fabric to wipe away the moisture dripping down her cheek.

"Have you eaten?"

She shook her head, not trusting the sound of her voice at that moment.

He reached for the tray, setting it at her side while he positioned himself in front of her, crossed legged.

"Why don't we start with some fruit?" He picked up an apple wedge, placing it between her unresponsive lips.

"I want you to eat, Lynn." His words were soft but held all the command of a man who expected to be obeyed.

She took a bite of the offered fruit, chewing its sweetness until it dissolved in her mouth. The reaction in her stomach was instantaneous.

"It would appear that your body is hungry even if you're too stubborn to want to eat," he said, feeding her the remainder of the fruit before picking up another item.

She wasn't sure how long they sat that way, with him hand feeding her until she couldn't eat another bite. It was a good thing, because between the both of them they'd polished off the majority of the items on the tray.

"Lay down." He set the tray aside, reaching into the drawer of the night stand.

Lynn lay back on the pillows, staring at the shiny red fabric in his hands.

"Give me your arm."

Their eyes locked for several silent moments before she offered up one limb, watching as he took his time securing one strip of smooth cloth around her wrists. He shoved several pillows aside to reveal a series of small posts that held the bed's high head board in place. He secured the opposite end of the fabric to one of the posts.

"Your other arm," he ordered, and Lynn thought a little longer over his request this time. Her heart pounded so hard in her chest that she could hear it thundering in her ears.

"Your arm, Lynn."

She held it out to him and waited for what was to come next. He made quick work, fastening her free arm.

"So, how long am I supposed to stay like this?" She finally spoke, glad that the ropes gave enough for her to bend her elbows.

This time he was silent, which was a bit unnerving.

"You have to understand that Logan needed my help and…and…" Her words trailed off as she became distracted by a hand on her knee. He trailed fingers lightly up her thigh, giving it a gentle squeeze.

"They are my family, I…"

His fingers dipped between her inner thighs this time, inching up further until he caressed the folds of her labia. He spread her legs to rest one on his denim clad thigh. She became increasingly aware that he sat fully dressed while she lay splayed in nothing save the satin straps at her wrist. Jake took care to make sure she was comfortable, angling pillows underneath her head, which served to give her full view of him touching her naked body.

His hand retreated back to her thigh, making her aware that she'd been holding her breath. This time he reached long arms up her torso until his thumb could trace the outline of her lips.

"You have always been very beautiful to me, Lynn. It's ridiculous to think of how many years I've pictured you lying before me."

He caressed her chin, down the length of her neck, stroking the outline of her collarbone, brushing knuckles over each breast. Her eyes drifted shut while she absorbed the erotic moment.

"Look at me." He tweaked one breast. Her eyes snapped open as she arched her back in pleasure. He continued plumping the nipple, only to add to her agony by pressing his other palm against her mound.

A barely audible sigh escaped from her lips.

"I always knew you would be this responsive to my touch," he said, adding pressure to his rotation.

Lynn tried to focus on what was being said, wanted to hear his admission of attraction, but his damned hands were driving her crazy.

He dipped his thumb between her folds, finding her clit. He applied firm pressure to his circular motions.

"Oh, God." She thrust her hips into the air, wanting more of his sweet teasing.

"You're so wet," he said, dipping first one finger, then a second between her wet vaginal walls.

"Yesss." She pushed into him as his mouth replaced fingers on her breast. He sucked the dark nipple into his lips, flicking it with his tongue. Fingers plundered her slick channel as his thumb continued the circular motion on her clit.

Lynn's breathing became ragged, and she could feel the sweet pressure building inside of her. God how she wished he would hurry and undress! As much as she enjoyed his fingers she wanted to feel him thick and hard inside of her.

"Damn," she groaned at the restraints that prevented her from touching him. He kissed a path down the length of her stomach, stopping at her pelvis. Fingers retreated from her now writhing body.

"Would you like me to continue?"

"Please," she begged, grateful when he slid down between her thighs. He spread her folds with his fingers, his head dipped down, tongue darting out to stroke her inflamed clit. He licked at the distended flesh several times until her toes dug into the mattress.

She was so close now, could feel the throes of the orgasm ready to consume her.

"I think we've had enough for one evening." He pulled away.

"No," Lynn moaned, certain that he was only teasing her now. She watched as he stood, waiting for him to remove those damnable clothes. She could see the engorged outline of his cock through the jeans and knew he wanted her just as much as she needed him.

"You've had a busy day, try and rest up now." He scooped up the tray before exiting the room.

Lynn thought he would return, that this was all his idea of a joke. Seconds ticked into minutes, and still more minutes. Gradually her heated body returned to normal although the frustrated tension hung in the background until sleep mercifully claimed her.

"Lynn," the distant voice called again, pulling her from the ebbing dream.

She opened her eyes slowly only to see his face hovering inches above her own.

"What now?" she moaned, turning her face into the downy pillow.

"Look at me."

She did, slowly rolling onto her bare back, grateful to discover he'd removed her binding while she slept. Was he back for round two of torture, she wondered wearily. He was just as naked as she. His cock stood at full attention.

"Sweetling, the last thing I wanted to do was punish you."

He could have fooled her.

"Now I think it's time I give us both what we really want." He trailed thick, work roughened fingers up her soft stomach, underneath one round breast.

Dear God, if he left her in another state of aroused frustration she wouldn't be held responsible for her actions. Ways of executing revenge faded rapidly as his hands reawakened her body. How she wanted to be angry with him, to tell him where he could go with his Dominate/submissive crap. But, God help her, she wanted him just as he was. Most of all, she wanted to belong to him, to give herself to him in a way she'd never done with any other man.

* * * *

Jake had watched her slumbering form for several minutes before finally waking the beautiful sleeping woman. He hated leaving her in her earlier state, had wanted nothing more than to plunge into her tight sheath and bring them both the completion they both so desperately needed. But, he couldn't let her actions go unaddressed.

Her blatant disregard of his request was the first of many things that afternoon that pissed him off. The next was finding her working side by side with the ranch hands, several of whom were more interested in watching her rear end then in paying attention to their tasks. Logan's territorial attitude only worsened things, as did Lynn's coming — yet again — to the man's rescue. By the time she'd finally capitulated to Jake's requests to get in the truck, his jovial mood of earlier had soured completely. The straw came when she'd disobeyed another of his edicts by not waiting for him as requested.

Now she lay before him, his brown-skinned queen ready to give herself to him. He wanted nothing more in his life than to have her. He knew once their two weeks ended he couldn't let her just walk away from him. No, he'd do whatever it took to keep her at his side.

He traced one darkly colored nipple with his thumb and watched as it immediately puckered. His gaze drifted up to hers and he could see the pleading in her eyes. She craved the feel of him inside her as much as he wanted to be there, stroking them to their climax.

"How much of yourself are you willing to give to me, Lynn?" The question was out before he'd had a chance to think about it. Would she understand what he was asking? Better still, would she be able to give herself to him completely.

Passion filled eyes as looked up at him. "Everything."

He inhaled deeply, his own heart pounding against his chest as he gripped her thighs in a firm hold, pulling her to him until he lay nestled between her thighs. How he wished he could be sure she meant what she uttered, not just because her body begged for release.

"Show me, open wide for me. Give me all you got."

And to their sheer joy, she did.

Six

"Are you up to making one of your fabulous meals for a few extra people tonight?" Jake asked in a late morning call.

"I might be able to swing that." Lynn swiveled away from the computer, unable to prevent the smile that spread across her face at the sound of his voice. "Exactly how many?"

"About five or six. My foremen and their ladies."

"All right, I'll see what I can whip up."

"Whatever it is, I'm sure it will be wonderful."

Her smile broadened.

"We're going to call it quits early today, so I should be home around four."

"I assume that means I won't see you for lunch?"

"As much as I hate it, yes," he sighed. His obvious disappointment lessened her own.

"So later it is."

"Around four-thirty," he promised before ending the call.

No sooner were they off the phone Lynn was kitchen bound to see what she could make to feed eight people. She was pleased to find all the ingredients for a meatloaf and mashed potatoes meal, complete with a broccoli and cheese casserole and homemade rolls. Her mother's famous peach cobbler would finish the meal nicely, she decided, completing her checklist. When Helen arrived at noon she enlisted the woman's help with that evenings meal and pitched in to get the outside company ready.

By the time Jake drug in after four, Lynn felt a huge sense of accomplishment with the completed tasks and a little like a conductor facilitating an orchestra of steaming pots and pans which would add finality to her busy day.

"Smells good in here." He dipped to give her lips a light brush as she filled a second baking pan with freshly cooked peaches.

"Thanks." In work mode she tried not to let herself get distracted by the rugged, sexy look he had going on twenty-four-seven. "You never said what time everyone would be arriving."

"I told them to make it here a little before six."

She nodded absently, thinking that would be just enough time to allow her to run upstairs for a quick shower and change while the pies baked.

"You've outdone yourself."

"Would you like to sample anything, I can make you a taste plate."

"Sweetling, what I want is not cooking on that stove at the moment."

That got her attention, causing her to blush profusely despite the very intimate nature of their relationship.

"Perhaps I should take you upstairs and remind you just how appetizing I find you."

Dammit, she couldn't believe he was getting her wet with just the mere suggestion of a sexual distraction.

She cleared her throat, not caring that he knew how effected she was. "We could, but then when your guests start to arrive in about an hour they'll think your woman wasn't ready for them."

Oh, hell, why had she just said that, she berated herself. Maybe Jake would ignore her little slip of the tongue. At least, she hoped as she busied herself with cutting strips for her crust.

"My woman. I like the sound of that."

Was he serious? She wanted to question him, to ask for an explanation of what he liked about the idea of her being his. Was he just talking in terms temporary sex? Unfortunately, the words wouldn't bring themselves to roll off her tongue.

"I'm going to get showered. If you change your mind come on up."

"Okay," was all she could manage. For a split second she thought Jake hesitated, but the second didn't last and within moments she found herself alone again.

* * * *

His employees were more than that. They were friends. Some of the men and their partners looked instantly familiar. Two of the foremen were just a little older than her, and had actually been to The Harrington a few times with her brothers in their youth. One other man she recognized after he'd made a point of reminding her that they were in the same graduating class. Steven Clark, she remembered him—all through high school he was an arrogant son of a bitch who thought women lived just for his pleasure. Apparently, he was married now and the papa of four. She couldn't help but wonder what type of woman could have saddled herself to him. He'd come alone that evening because his wife stayed behind to care for their sick twins. Lynn almost rolled her eyes when he offered up the explanation for her absence. Poor woman at home with two ill children, and two others barely out of diapers. She would make sure to pack her some leftovers, complete with a big helping of desert.

They started with pre-dinner drinks on the deck, and Lynn was completely immersed in the stories each person regaled about the other, especially the ones that gave her more insight into Jake. What he hadn't already told her about the eleven years they'd spent apart she learned that evening. Although Jake hadn't spent the time womanizing, he was far from a saint, she discovered. Lynn laughed over tales of women who'd snuck out to the ranch or shown up at the site in the hopes of enticing the attractive, wealthy bachelor. She felt completely at ease with the group, even found herself joining in on the good natured teasing.

Dinner was served in the formal dinning room, although there was nothing formal about the friendly atmosphere. Throughout the evening Lynn caught Jake's open stares and approving smiles, and couldn't help but wonder what he was thinking.

"Okay, Rangell, you've stalled long enough," Beth, the wife of an older foreman, said as they enjoyed dessert back on the roomy deck. Hoots and hollers from several members of the group had Lynn looking around, perplexed.

"Leave the man alone, Beth Anne. I swear, he's gon' fire me one day just to keep you at bay," her husband joked.

"Jake loves it and you know it. There's no way a man could move like he does and not enjoy it, isn't that right, Jake?"

What the hell were they going on about? Lynn quirked an eyebrow at Jake for clarification, only to get a broad toothy grin.

"You just love the fact that he can keep up with you," this from another wife.

"Okay, does someone want to tell me what you're talking about?" Lynn finally asked, her gaze jumping from various faces as she waited for a response.

"The two-step, dearie," Beth volunteered. "I swear this man of yours is the best in all of Texas.

Jake! She wasn't sure what she was expecting, but it wasn't that.

"You're kidding me, right?" she asked no one in particular while she studied Jake's face for an answer.

"I do, alright," he finally added.

"Oh, stop being modest when we all know you're anything but," Beth Ann joked. "Now, are you going to keep sitting there teasing me or are we going to dance?"

"Just for a little bit," he agreed, getting up to start an outdoor radio completely concealed in a hideaway compartment on the deck.

"You're in for a treat," Beth said with confidence as she and Jake moved to an open area.

All he needs is a cowboy hat to complete the look, she thought as he and Beth moved around the floor. Pretty soon a few others joined in, turning the two-person dance into a line. Lynn sat back in her chair, enjoying the performance. They were all good, but Jake…maybe it was just her bias, but she thought he was great.

"Didn't believe the old man had it in him like that until I saw it for myself."

Lynn wasn't sure when Steven sidled up next to her, but there he was sitting in the chair that Jake had recently occupied.

"Yeah, I must admit I'm a little surprised," she answered, not taking her eyes off the group.

"Hmm, life is full of surprises, I'm coming to learn. Take you and Jake, for instance."

That got her attention.

He didn't wait for a response before continuing. "I would have never thought that the two of you would hook up, but I guess everything has a price."

Lynn restrained herself as she fixed a steady gaze on him.

"Price?"

"Hmm, maybe that was the wrong choice of words. I'm sure yours and Jake's arrangement is a mutually beneficial one. Although, I must say I think Jake is getting the better deal from all of this. Personally, I don't think there is any oil where your brother is planning to drill. If you ask me…"

"I think I've heard enough of your opinions for one evening." Lynn cut him off before making what she hoped was a dignified exit. On shaky legs she made her way into the house, not sure what to do next. Her first instinct was to leave, end it all. Just grab a set of keys and lick her wounds all the way back to The Harrington. Instead, she made her way to the kitchen where she busied herself with cleaning up their dinner mess. She needed something to do with her herself that wouldn't get her locked up for committing homicide.

That bastard, she thought, but wasn't certain if it were Steven or Jake she referred to.

Part of her wanted to believe that Steven was just guessing, but he seemed to be right on the money with everything. Did everyone know why they were together? Hell, hadn't he told her that he mentioned to some about her temporary stay? She guessed she should have questioned him at the time. What an idiot! Now what?

Lynn was near tears as her mind raced with possibilities while she scrubbed dishes and counter tops. Her fervor only seemed to increase with each passing minute. Her heart was breaking. It was foolish that after only a few days with him she'd let herself get so caught up. Ultimately this was all a business arrangement, and she'd gone and fallen for Jake Rangell.

"This couldn't have waited until later?"

The deep, irritated sound of Jake's voice resonated in the quiet kitchen, causing Lynn to jump. She'd been so distracted she neither heard nor saw when he entered in what should have been plain sight.

NIA K. FOXX

"It's late, and I'm developing a bit of a headache, so I thought it better to get it all done now," she answered, giving the already gleaming surface of the island an extra cleaning. She was glad for something other than him to focus on.

"Did something happen? Steven didn't say anything he shouldn't have?"

She shook her head in denial. "Just friendly conversation."

Jake stayed rooted to his position while he studied her. "Are you attempting to wipe a hole in the counter?"

"I didn't want to leave a mess for Helen tomorrow," she answered easily.

"You know *that* is what I pay her for."

Why wouldn't he just leave, go back to his friends, and share more of her private life?

"Yes, I'm well aware of everyone's position here."

"What is that supposed to mean, Lynn?" He closed the distance in a couple of long strides. When she would have moved away he trapped her between the counter and his body.

"It's not important. If you wouldn't mind too much I'd like to turn in early tonight. I don't think my headache will improve." She let the lie slip easily from her lips, hating herself for enjoying being so close to him.

"Look at me," he ordered, and her first response was to protest, but the tone in his voice had her following a less rebellious thought.

His eyes searched hers as if seeking their own answers.

106

"If you need something for this convenient headache, there's Tylenol in the cabinet, but know this: you will stay by my side until our last guest leaves. Afterwards, we'll discuss what's bothering you. Is that understood?"

"Yes," she answered a little too meekly for her liking.

Damn...damn...why can't I just tell him to kiss my black ass and march right out the front door. She berated herself taking Jake's offered hand. *Because you're a dick whipped wimp, with a weak spot for Alpha males. Hell, with a weak spot for him specifically.*

Jake wasn't kidding when he said he wanted her at his side the remainder of the evening, going so far as to shift their chairs closer to one another when they rejoined their visitors. He eased her hand into his own while they continued chatting. The pad of his thumb gingerly rubbed the top of her hand in a soothing pattern. If anyone noticed the additional affection no one made a public acknowledgement. In the background a variety of country, soft rock, and Motown hummed on, and in spite of everything Lynn found herself relaxing again.

Steven was the first to say his goodbyes, and she could honestly say that she was happy to see him go. There was definitely truth in the saying about the bearers of bad news.

"I hear it told that you all are about to start your own drilling venture on The Harrington," Greg, Jake's senior foremen, stated.

Her body's reaction was instant. So much for relaxation.

"Yes, but we're not looking to delve too deeply into the industry. The Harrington is and always will be a cattle ranch," she responded smoothly, proud of herself for the unwavering pattern in her voice. Lynn could feel Jake's eyes on her as she tried to gently tug her hand free from his grasp. He wasn't having it.

"It's a good thing you decided to come home, because that place was looking a right mess. For awhile there I heard talk of it being sold."

"Well, I'm sure we all know how unreliable rumors can be."

Greg nodded his head in agreement, "Very true."

"If I gave much credence to gossip, hun, we probably wouldn't be married right now," Beth Anne piped up, giving her husband's knee an affectionate pat.

"Well, I'm glad you didn't."

"And I'm certain your children feel the same way," Jake provided.

Lynn was glad to have the spotlight off her family.

"Speaking of gossip, is it true that your Anthony is going up to Princeton?" another of the guests questioned.

"Sure is, but I don't know why he couldn't just go to Texas A&M." Greg shook his head in genuine bewilderment.

Lynn bit back her smile. Spoken like a true Texan.

"Dance with me." She'd barely had a chance to register his request before Jake was pulling her to her feet, guiding her to the makeshift dance space the group used earlier.

Aretha Franklin's *Natural Woman* played in the background, and she almost groaned aloud at how true the Queen of Soul's words were to her situation. In Jake she'd found everything she was looking for in a man. He was the epitome of strength, passion, caring, raw sexual energy, intelligence and to top it all off he was a natural Dom—not just some guy hiding behind a title to get his thrills. With him she didn't have to hide her own submissive nature.

They swayed smoothly to the slow melody, bodies pressed so closely there was scarce room for anything but their breathing. Their eyes were drawn to each other in silent communication. She wondered if he knew the dedication her heart was sending out with each note. She should have seen the kiss coming, probably did see it but chose to pretend ignorance until their lips connected. The lingering hurt she felt over Steven's revelation was pushed to the back of her mind with his coaxing lips. She welcomed his probing tongue in her mouth, enjoying the taste and feel of him. It all ended much too soon for her, and apparently him as well because Lynn felt his hesitation when he finally raised his head.

"Well, look at the time," Lynn vaguely registered someone saying.

"We should really be going," the female's voice was a lot clearer and sounded very amused.

"Your friends are leaving," Lynn whispered.

"Perhaps we should see them to the door."

"Seems like the proper thing to do."

* * * *

"I'm so glad you and Jake are together," Beth Anne said, giving Lynn a brief embrace at the front door.

"Thank you," she said, although the woman's words only served to remind her of the reality of their relationship.

"You know, we should feel bad for letting everyone leave so soon," she told Jake as they closed the door on the last person.

"Hmm, maybe." Jake pulled her into his arms again. He gave her lips a quick kiss. "I think it's time we talked about what upset you earlier."

"There's nothing to talk about, Jake."

"You're a terrible liar, sweetling. Now we can do this the easy way or the hard one. The choice is yours." As he spoke he secured both her arms behind her with one of his own. Although his hold was firm it was far from painful.

His eyes narrowed at her silence. "I'm sure you remember how I treat defiance, Lynn."

Hell, yeah, she remembered the sweet torture, and could go forever without a repeat of that frustration.

"Steven apparently knows about our arrangement," she admitted.

He had the nerve to look genuinely perplexed. "How?"

"You don't know?" She didn't try to hide the accusatory tone in her voice.

"You can't honestly think I confided in him."

"How else would he have known if he hadn't been told?"

"I don't know, Lynn, but I haven't divulged the specifics of our living arrangement to anyone. As far as my people are concerned we are in a relationship of our own making."

"But Steven—"

"...is an asshole who was grasping at straws. Do you honestly believe I would confide in him?"

"No," she answered honestly. Jake hadn't actually said more than a couple words to the man all evening.

"Good, then we'll ignore this incident. Unless you want him fired, just say the word."

"Of course I don't want that. I wouldn't want to punish his family for him."

"I'm glad to hear it. Now, can we put this behind us?"

She nodded. "I'm sorry that I assumed the worse."

"As you should be." His eyes twinkled mischievously. "Perhaps you're ready to show me just how sorry you are."

She didn't need to clarify his meaning. "Yes, I am."

The hand holding her arms in place dropped, but she intertwined her fingers behind her back to maintain her submissive position. Sinking silently to her knees, she held his gaze, allowing her eyes to fall briefly as she posed the question they both knew was coming next.

"May I touch you?"

He paused briefly. "Where?"

"Your cock." God, how she felt brazen saying the word. Her body warmed at the very thought of taking him in her mouth, something she hadn't had the pleasure of doing yet. Jake had been a very generous lover, demanding little.

"Hmm, and exactly what would you like to do to it, sweetling?"

"I'd prefer to show you."

"Then proceed."

With deft fingers she leisurely unbuckled his jeans, taking pleasure in his sharp intake of breath when she finally released his semi-erect cock. She stroked his sac, before encircling the burgeoning thickness of his shaft. At Jake's low groan she kissed the head of his penis, swirling her tongue around its opening before sinking her warm mouth over him.

* * * *

Jake had never felt anything so blissfully intoxicating as her swallowing him. He couldn't tear his gaze away from the picture of thick lips stroking up and down his length. She was tormenting him on purpose, had to be, the way she gradually consumed him.

"I love the way you feel," he moaned, sinking a hand into her soft hair.

His cock strained beyond belief, and he wanted nothing more than to take her right there on the floor of the foyer. His legs nearly buckled when she massaged his sac while pumping him further in her mouth, taking him to the back of her throat.

He fought to maintain control over his stimulated cock, but found it a losing battle as her mouth contracted around him, slurping him.

"I'm going to cum, baby," he tried to warn, tugging her hair in case she hadn't understood his rough words. The declaration seemed to spur her on even more. Her head bobbed over him in enthusiastic repetition — devouring, sucking, and retracting until he could no longer stave off the inevitable.

"Lynn," he barked as a final caution.

Too late, he thought. His cocked throbbed as he filled her mouth with every ounce of his seed. Greedily she gulped it down, only to continue sucking him off until he had nothing left to offer her.

She sat back on her haunches, looking up at him from under hooded eyes, licking her lips clean. He'd never seen anything more beautiful before in his life.

"Am I forgiven?" she asked humbly.

"God, yes." If he'd truly been upset he would have been able to forgive her most anything. He helped her to her feet before giving her another deep kiss that left her gasping for breath. Aroused nipples stabbed at his chest and it was his turn to look like the cat that swallowed the cannery, because he knew that before the night was out he would bring her the same pleasure.

Seven

Albeit unorthodox, Lynn admitted she enjoyed the relationship that was developing between her and Jake. Over the last few days they'd fallen into a pattern, with Jake working on the ranch most mornings while she continued getting his financial statements organized. By afternoon he was home, ready for lunch and extracurricular activities that left her breathless. She found his voracious sexual appetite matched her growing one. Ways of pleasing her very dominant partner seemed to be at the forefront of her thoughts on a daily basis. She knew whatever pleasure he derived from their encounters they would be reciprocated ten-fold.

In fact, she had one particular idea in motion that day. When Jake walked through the front door that afternoon, he would be in for a very sensuous surprise. She'd called Helen earlier, giving the woman the day off, not caring if she had to pay her salary out of her own pocket.

She'd spent the morning after Jake left transforming his family room into a pleasure palace, pushing the two lightweight sofas to one end of the room and sliding partitions in place to obscure their presence. She went about the house looking for any decorative pillows she could get her hands on.

Surprisingly she found plenty and made a mental note to question Jake about who'd been involved in decorating his house.

She knew that he'd had his share of lovers, had most likely brought them to his bed, but the thought of someone being so close to him that she would leave a bit of herself in his home décor unsettled her. Although Lynn reminded herself that their arrangement was coming to an end she couldn't help but think of Jake as her man, and she didn't want thoughts of another woman intruding in on their time together. Soon enough she would be back at The Harrington working side by side with her brothers, but until that moment she would content herself with the fantasy of having Jake Rangell all to herself.

She laid out a bowl of fresh fruits she'd sliced, and tightly closed all the blinds, which effectively blocked light out of the room. Although the days were warm, she lit the fireplace for ambiance before heading upstairs to prepare herself.

Freshly showered and scented, she donned her white silk robe and added the final touch to her seduction, a CD full of instrumental middle-eastern melodies just perfect for the occasion.

She checked the wall clock, it would be just a short time before he arrived. She loosened her robe, allowing it to drape slightly open in the front to reveal her ample cleavage.

"Honey, I'm home," Jake called from the foyer some minutes later.

Lynn couldn't stop the grin that spread across her entire face. With the exuberance of a child on

Christmas morning, she bounded down the hall to where he was.

"I've been waiting for you," she answered, slowing her gait as she rounded the corner.

Jake stood ogling her for several seconds before cursing under his breath.

"I have a surprise for you," she said, unable to resist the urge to kiss him. At his unenthusiastic response she pulled back, perplexed. "What?"

"I have a surprise for you, too, but I think I'd much prefer if you were showing a little less flesh," he answered as he readjusted the lapels on her robe, then tightened the sash to keep it in place.

"What's going on?" She searched his eyes.

"That's exactly what I would like to know Twittle." Although less boisterous than it had been in her youth, there was no mistaking the voice of Race Harrington emanating from behind Jake.

Lynn groaned, wishing there was a hole she could find quickly and crawl into.

"Daddy?" she called, gripping the front of Jake's shirt. Maybe she'd heard incorrectly.

No such luck. "Stop hiding behind that man and come greet your daddy properly, young lady."

"Do I have to?" she muttered to herself, already stepping around Jake and putting on the bravest face she could muster.

She hesitated at the sight that greeted her. Not only was Race present in the wheelchair he'd been confined to for the past two years since his stroke, but her brother Ryan pushed him further into the foyer, trailed by a stone faced Logan.

"What are you doing here?" she croaked, not sure which man she was addressing.

"I'd like to know the same thing, but I gather from the way you're dressed I already know," Race continued as his daughter brushed a brief kiss on his cheek.

"Maybe we've come at a bad time," Ryan spoke up, perusing her silk clad body, though he made no move to leave.

"I'd say this is the perfect time," Race continued. "Now, Twittle, why don't you go change into something more presentable? We'll wait for you in the..." He looked to Jake, who stood only inches behind her quietly taking in the scene unfolding in front of him.

"Family room," he offered.

"No! Why don't you all wait in the sitting room," Lynn squealed before turning to run up the stairs.

She took her time dressing, going over a series of scenarios that would explain her stepfather's presence down stairs. Her final conclusion involved Logan spilling the beans since he couldn't convince her to terminate her agreement with Jake. Now dressed in her staple ranch attire of blue jeans and button-up shirt, she made her way downstairs. She was relieved to see that Jake had heeded her suggestion.

Race sat with Ryan at his side, while Logan stood in front of a bay window, seemingly lost in thought while he gazed out. Lynn noted that Jake looked calm sitting opposite her stepfather and brothers as if he were a silent observer. She hated the eerie silence that engulfed the room.

"You're looking well today, Daddy," she said, trying to decide where she would sit for this conversation. There was one empty chair adjacent her father and one next to Jake.

"Why don't you sit down, Twittle?" Race instructed.

"I think I'd much rather stand." She deduced there was less risk of causing more strain in the room than if she chose a seat.

"Sit down, Lynn," Jake insisted, indicating the chair next to his own. Their eyes locked for several tense moments before she acquiesced.

"What are you doing here, Daddy?" she ventured again, looking between her two brothers. Logan continued to stare out the window as if she hadn't spoken. Ryan settled into his chair for what promised to be an interesting discussion. She hated the anticipation in his eyes.

"I believe that is my question to you." Her father quirked a brow in her direction.

"He heard about the incident at The Harrington," Logan provided as if talking to himself.

"Yes, and imagine my surprise to know that my daughter was still in Texas and staying at the Rangell Ranch, no less. From what I hear, told Jake came after you as if he had some claim on you, Twittle?"

"Well, I think that's a little exaggerated," she supplied with nervous laughter.

"I don't know. I heard several of the men say that Jake ordered you in his truck and that he and

Logan nearly came to blows out there," Ryan provided.

Lynn gave her older brother a look that promptly silenced him. Leave it to Ryan to find amusement in the unfolding drama.

"Jake isn't denying that the two of you have been involved, but I think that's fairly obvious," her father continued.

Lynn couldn't prevent the sigh of relief from escaping. So he didn't know about their little subterfuge. As far as he was concerned she'd been sneaking around with Jake Rangell. It wasn't good, but she could live with it.

"The question is, what do you plan to do to rectify the damage done?" Race pinned Jake with ice blue eyes.

"Hold on a second, Daddy," she broke in. "There is nothing to be done, Jake and I are two consenting adults."

"It's all right, Lynn, your father has every right to question my intentions." Jake silenced her with a reassuring hand.

She didn't like how this was turning out. Lynn looked to her two brothers for help but Logan hadn't budged. Ryan looked as if he had front row seats at NASCAR.

"And just for your peace of mind, Mr. Harrington, I plan on making an honest woman of your daughter just as soon as humanly possible."

"What?" Both she and Logan exclaimed in unison.

"Paw, I thought we were just going to come here and bring Lynn home," Logan nearly roared.

"A wrong has to be corrected," Race informed.

"It looks like we gon' have ourselves a shotgun weddin'," Ryan guffawed with an exaggerated southern accent.

"Stop being such a redneck, Ryan," Lynn admonished.

"Let's get this clear," Jake said, leaning in, resting forearms on his knees. "I'm marrying Lynn because it's what I want, not because of any perceived coercion."

"Now just wait a minute," Lynn looked between every man in the room. "Who said anything about marriage? This isn't the fifties or sixties, and I won't marry any man because of some false sense of propriety."

"I agree with Lynn," Logan piped in. "We just need to get her home."

"Stay out of it, Logan." Jake's soft tone held a menace that sent shivers down her spine.

"I'll go home—"

"Lynn," Jake's voice held a warning all its own.

"—when I'm good and ready. Daddy," she said more gently, now coming to kneel in front of the man who'd been there for every scrapped knee, teasing, and fight over the last twenty-four years. "I'm sorry that I lied to you, I just didn't think you would understand."

"How could you not think I wouldn't understand about love, Twittle? Your mother has been gone for six years, but do you think I miss or love her any less? She and I overcame obstacles you children will never understand, to be together in a time when people weren't as accepting as they are today." His blue eyes softened. "But I would do it all over again to have her in my arms."

Tears that she hadn't known were there rolled down her face over the declaration of love.

"I think it's time I told you children the truth about the conflict between our families."

Lynn could feel Jake stiffening behind her. "It's okay, Daddy."

"No, it's hung between us long enough, might as well get it out in the open if you and Jake are going to have a future together."

"About that…" She couldn't let him believe that something permanent was on the rise between Jake and her.

"Sit down, Lynn, and let your father speak his peace," Jake said from behind her. The tight strain in his voice wasn't lost on her.

She worried her bottom lip for several seconds before pushing to her feet and reclaiming her seat next to him.

"Before Kathleen died she felt the need to unburden her poor soul to me. Guess she wanted meet our maker with a clear conscience."

He started, directing at Lynn. "When your biological father was still alive, your mother had a brief affair with Jake's father."

"What?" The collective question went up around the room.

"She said that neither of them meant for it to happen, but they'd been attracted to each other for years. Your fathers were good friends, and it tore Jake's dad up inside to be in love with his friend's wife. One night when Lynn was just a little girl, her parents had a terrible fight and Kathleen left her husband. Tom was the one to find her. He tried to encourage her to come home to her family, but she was still too upset. He spent most of the night listening to her pour her heart out over her husband, even held her while she cried. I guess it was a combination of things that night, but the result ended with Kathleen and Tom spending the night together in the biblical sense." Race paused to clear his throat.

"He never said anything," Jake whispered.

He directed his next revelation to Jake. "At any rate, your mother found out first and went to Lynn's father with the news. It was the day of his accident."

"Dear God," Lynn mumbled.

"Despite his affair with Kathleen, your father loved your mother very much, but he also loved Lynn's mother. After the death of her husband the two stayed away from each other, both racked with guilt that they were responsible for the accident."

"But he attacked Kathleen when Lynn was just a little girl. Don't you remember?" Jake asked, turning to a stunned Lynn who merely nodded.

Race continued, nodding as if Jake had addressed him. "Kathleen said there was more to the events of the day she left. She'd come to Tom asking for help to leave but he refused. He wanted her with him even if it meant only living under the same roof. He pleaded with her and it broke her heart. She cried. They were kissing when Lynn came in, and her mother was the first to see her. She tried to push Tom away, not wanting her child to see the two of them together, with Lynn's Paw just dying she was already very confused about things. Your father didn't see Lynn, and when he wouldn't turn Kathleen loose it must have frightened the girl. As things tend to do, the situation escalated and Kathleen screamed at him. You came running, and well, you know the rest."

"I'd always thought him crazy for his obsession with her. I didn't know there was actual history to it," Jake said thoughtfully.

"Things are usually not what they appear on the surface," Race reaffirmed. "You come home when you're ready, Twittle, just don't make me wait until next week. I'm sure you two have many things to discuss." The elder Harrington tapped Ryan's arm, signaling time for their departure. "Come on, boys, it looks like we're done here."

"What about Lynn?" Logan looked anxious.

"Oh, give it up already Logan," Ryan said, rising to his feet. "What you need is to go to town and meet a nice girl. Frankly, it's a little sick the way you obsess over Lynn. I don't care if she is our stepsister, she's still family."

The room went silent for several moments before Race burst into laughter. "I thought I was the only one who noticed it."

The shocked look on Lynn's face spoke volumes, and she watched as Logan turned several shades of red before stalking out of the room.

She stood to give her stepfather a goodbye kiss, her mind abuzz with all the revelations.

"I guess it wouldn't be right of me to say I told ya so," Jake said, encircling her waist to pull her back against his solid body.

"So I guess this means we're having a wedding?" Ryan asked as the couple followed them into the foyer.

"You can count on it," Jake answered without pause.

"We'll get back to you on that one," Lynn countered.

"I believe that counts as disobedience, my little submissive," Jake whispered in her ear as the two remaining members of her family followed Logan to the waiting truck.

"So, what surprise do you have for me in the family room?" Jake turned her in his arms as soon as the door closed behind their guests.

"Jake, I think we need to talk."

"About what?" he said before giving her a lingering kiss.

For a moment she forgot what she'd been about to say. "About this whole marriage business, what my father just told us. Take your pick."

"As far as what happened between our parents this answers a lot of unasked questions, but it doesn't change things between us."

What us? She silently wondered. Their time together was nearly up and he'd never made any mention of them continuing their relationship.

"You smell delicious," Jake mumbled against her neck, bringing her back to the present.

"We're not getting married," she exhaled gradually as her body began to hum with excitement.

"No?" he reared back slightly, capturing her gaze. "Did you think I was really going to let you go at the end of the week?"

She nodded, missing his closeness. "It's what we agreed to."

"I believe you're the one who informed me that I'm an unscrupulous business man. I'm prepared to give your family back their land and livestock if you agree to stay with me."

Her eyes rounded at his admission. "For how long?"

He shrugged, "Indefinitely."

"So why not just ask me?"

This time he paused as if the thought were a completely new one.

"Would you stay?"

"Maybe, if I were asked properly...hey." She giggled as all six-foot-three of him bent on one knee in front of her.

"Will you stay, be my wife, build a happy home with me, and fill these empty rooms with children and the halls with laughter?" His sober gaze held hers.

Lynn's heart stopped at his heartfelt request.

"Dear God, yes." A fresh batch of tears filled her eyes. So much for the thin layer of eyeliner she applied for her earlier seduction.

"When?"

"I don't know." Everything was moving so fast. "Whenever."

"This weekend." He rose to his feet, pulling her down the hall to the family room.

"You can't be serious."

"I've never been more serious about anything before in my life." He paused, giving her a thoughtful backwards look before taking her the remainder of the way into the room.

"Wow!" he exclaimed, getting his first real glimpse at the transformation.

"You like?" she asked, taking in his stunned expression.

"How could I not?" He stepped into the dimly lit room where the fire blazed with full force. The music set on auto repeat continued to fill the tranquil space.

"You did all this?"

"All by my lonesome. By the way, I gave Helen the day off with pay. I hope that's okay?"

"More than okay." He turned his back on the seductive atmosphere. "Now, if I remember correctly, this setting required you to be partially clothed."

"Actually," she unbuttoned her blouse leisurely. "It called for me to be completely nude."

"Do tell?"

She let the blouse slip into a puddle at her feet, followed by her bra and jeans. She pivoted to give him full rear view as she slid panties over her rounded rear and down thick thighs. She twirled her hips in a slow rhythmic pattern to the music. Her movements would have made any video vixen envious.

"Mercy, woman."

She rotated to face him again, "Let me do that." She grasped his hands as he attempted to remove his gray T-shirt. With minimal assistance she managed to discard his dusty clothes, taking time to stack the items in a neat pile by the door, if only to frustrate him further.

"Please lay down, Sir." She indicated the pillow arrangement on the floor in front of the large hearth. Jake did so in his typical suave fashion, arms behind his head as he reclined on the plumped pillows with legs crossed.

"Would Sir like some fruit to quench his hunger?"

He nodded, his hooded eyes watching her intentionally seductive movements. Lynn placed the bowl at her side as she knelt in front of him, feeling every bit the submissive servant tending to her Dom.

"Does Sir have a preference of fruit?"

"Surprise me."

She started with an orange wedge, placing the juicy fruit between his lips. Lord, he looked sexy laying there in all his splendor. Her gaze raked his body smiling as his aroused cock jumped under her gaze.

"More," he said, bringing her attention back to his face.

Lynn fed him one piece of fruit after the next, surprised at how doing so effected her body's responses.

"Touch your breasts," Jake commanded, eyes resting on the heavy orbs.

She cupped each breast, massaging slowly.

"Pinch your nipples for me."

Lynn complied, groaning at the self-inflicted pleasure.

"If I may, I would like to please Sir now."

"You may."

Lynn straddled his legs in one fluid motion, scratching nails up and down his legs and stomach like she'd come to know he liked.

"I have been negligent in giving pleasure to you, Sir, and I fully intend to rectify that mistake, else I be punished," she said, caressing his enlarged cock.

"Proceed," he authorized.

Lynn nodded obligingly. Dipping her head, she twirled her tongue around the head of his penis in a slow pattern, savoring the taste of him. Her mouth sank over the large staff, taking him to the back of her throat. His quick intake of air encouraged her further. She massaged his sac while alternating between swallowing him slow, fast, and slow again. Her mouth slurped in every inch she could accommodate.

She gazed up at him, watching the near pained look on his face as he fought the orgasm she knew was impending from her amorous attention.

"Enough," Jake grabbed a fistful of hair to stop her greedy mouth.

"Did I do something wrong, Sir?" she asked with mock concern, her tongue snaking out one last time to catch the fluid that trickled from his tip.

"Don't play coy with me, woman. I won't waste my cum in your mouth when I'd much rather fill you with it. I want you to ride me so that I can see those beautiful titties bouncing, and feel that sweet tight cunt sucking me dry."

Lynn's body throbbed beyond belief already but his words had her wet channel nearly dripping.

"As you wish."

She rose, prepared to mount and ride him as described, but Jake's next sentence stopped her as she hovered excitedly over him.

"First thing's first." He reached up for the patch on her arm, snatching the square adhesive from her skin and tossing it somewhere over his head. "I've wanted to do that since the first night."

Hands gripped her hips, slamming her down on his hard length, and Lynn threw her head back at the joy of finally having him within her. She braced her arms on his shoulders while grinding him inside her, working her steaming core around his thick heavy penis. The sound of pounding flesh and groans effectively drowned out the low melodic music. Lynn bit her lower lip as she raised completely off his throbbing cock before crashing back over him. She could feel her completion threatening to overtake her, but did her best to hold it at bay until...

"Mmm, that's it. Fuck me," Jake groaned. His orgasm hit him hard, fingers bit into her waist at his completing howl.

Her frenzied body found its own completion while he throbbed inside of her, milking him even more of his sticky fluid until his jumping cocked stilled inside her.

"Stay." Jake wrapped arms around her waist.

"I'm too heavy," she protested.

He gave her naked bottom a firm swat. "You're perfect, now don't argue."

She wasn't sure how long she lay listening to the steady thud of his hammering heart.

"There's something I want to tell you," she said, staving off the haze of sleep that threatened.

"Hmm."

"I need you to listen."

"I am."

She raised up, meeting his somber eyes. "I owe you an apology for my comment about your dad. I had no right…"

"It's all right. Besides, it doesn't change what he did after your mother left. My father wasn't a saint by anyone's standard, and he was downright obsessed where your mother was concerned. The day your mother died I never saw him grieve so much, not even for his own wife."

"I can't begin to imagine how they both must have felt during those earlier years, both married but wanting someone else," Lynn sighed.

"And as long as I live I'll make sure that we don't know that torture. I love you, Lynn, I want you to know that."

Her heart stopped.

"I've probably loved you since before I should, you need to know that going into this marriage and understand that I will do everything in my power to make you happy."

"I love you too, Jake."

"Please don't feel you have to—"

"Listen to me," she urged. "I've loved you forever, but thought it impossible for you to love me back. I spent years trying to get you off my mind, wanting to chalk my feelings up as a school girl crush. When you kissed me that day at the fair it gave me hope, but then you ignored me after that."

"I stayed away because I knew if I didn't I wouldn't be able to keep my hands off you."

"Well, you don't have to keep them off now. I've become quite accustomed to your touch, some might say that I crave."

"Ditto," he said, running hands down her back to settle on her firm rear end. He gave it a gentle squeeze before reaching for the expanse of her hips.

"What are you doing?" Lynn gasped when he lifted and lowered her over his thickening member.

"I'm showing you exactly how it will be for us over the next twenty years."

She took over the steady rhythm wondering how they both could be aroused so quickly. "Twenty? Is that the best you can do?"

She gasped as he easily switched their positions "Actually, more like thirty, forty tops. I didn't want to frighten you, but if you must know, us Rangell men are known for our fortitude," he informed before plunging deeply into her warmth.

Oh, she could believe it, and looked forward to the many years ahead of them.

Epilogue

"So are you two planning to stop having kids at some point?" Logan asked as they sat at the picnic table just behind her stepfather's home. He gave her rounded abdomen a gentle caress.

"We've both always wanted a big family, and considering Jake and I have gotten such a late start at it…" she shrugged, not completing her sentence.

"As long as you're happy," he said, looking out to the yard where a haphazard game of touch football was taking place. On one team were Jake, their three-year-old son Jefferson, and Logan's ten-year-old stepson Clint. The other team consisted of Ryan, the daughter of his most recent girlfriend, and said woman, whom they all agreed was a keeper.

"I am, are you?"

"Can't complain," Logan said, giving her a broad smile. "I guess you'll be the first in the family to know that Cheryl and I are pregnant."

"Congratulations," she said with enthusiasm, giving Logan a one-armed hug being careful not to disturb the sleeping baby in her other arm. "Who knows, maybe you two will catch up with us."

"Bite your tongue, woman."

"Now all we have to do is get that brother of ours to settle down," she sighed, looking at Ryan, who was doing more touching of his love interest and team member than playing football.

"Speaking of which, I have a confession to make," Logan looked from the open lawn that served as a field. "Jake didn't really swindle us out of the land, Ryan went to him."

"What?"

"Ryan told me right before you arrived, and I know I should have told you but I thought it would work to our benefit if you thought of Jake as a bastard."

"Why?"

"Because I was afraid of losing you to him. I knew how you'd felt about Jake all those years, and that your feelings were reciprocated. I just hoped your thinking he tricked us would be enough to keep him at arm's length."

"You're lucky I'm holding your niece, Logan Ambrose Harrington."

"I guess sorry isn't good enough."

"I'll get back to you on that, in the meantime you can start making it up to me by changing Jameela. Her bag is in my old room."

"You're kidding, right?"

She cocked her head, "Do I look like it?"

"All right, all right, might as well get the practice in while I can." He gently took the sleeping baby, cradling her as if she were the finest piece of china.

"Foul! Ryan I don't know how many times I have to tell you not to tag your own players," Race's voice boomed from the sidelines, causing Lynn to laugh.

Jake called a time out much to the chagrin of his son.

"Things looked pretty serious over here." He greeted her, straddling the seat Logan abandoned moments earlier.

"Nothing major, my brother just decided to enlighten me on the little matter of the land you bought from them. So why didn't you tell me that it was Ryan's idea?"

"It didn't matter, I knew I wouldn't keep it but thought it better I hold on to it until things got back to status quo over here instead of someone else swiping it up." He shrugged.

"I knew there was a reason why I loved you," she said, looking into his beautiful honeyed colored eyes.

"You needed a reason." He leaned in to give her a kiss that promised more to come later.

From the field Jefferson yelled, "Foul!"

About the Author

Nia Foxx is the author of several erotic romances. *The Rancher's Ultamatum* is her first title with Phaze. Readers may learn more about Nia's work through her website at http://www.niafoxx.com.

Printed in the United States
103958LV00006B/12/A